Journeys Through The Unknown

An anthology of supernatural adventures

by

Heather Beck

TREASURE COVE BOOKS

This book is a work of fiction. Names, places, events and characters are fictitious in every regard. Any similarities to actual events or persons, living or dead, are purely coincidental.

Journeys Through The Unknown
ISBN: 978-1-926990-04-0
Copyright © 2011 Heather Beck
Cover Photo Copyright © Kerri McClellan/Fotolia

Published by
Treasure Cove Books

Table of Contents:

Gnome Genome

Seventeen-year-old Meghan Bradford opened the sliding door that led to the backyard and walked onto the warm patio. It was a hot July morning and she planned to spend it relaxing on a hammock.

"The hammock," Meghan sighed, "is the only thing I like about this place."

Meghan and her family had just moved from a small prairie town to the city. The Bradfords were used to the beautiful scenery of an open landscape. Now that they lived in a two-story house, all they had to look at was their neighbor's backyard.

"It's all her fault," Meghan said aloud, while thinking about her mother. "If the bank hadn't promoted her to their headquarters, I'd be swimming in my pool right now."

Meghan approached the hammock and threw herself on it. Everything seemed to happen in slow motion as she felt her body tumble over and fall to the ground. Her head hit the ground with a sickening thud. For a moment, all she could see were red and yellow stars on a black background. However, her eyesight soon returned to normal, bringing with it a horrible headache.

"Are you alright?" someone shouted.

1

Meghan rubbed the side of her head and then looked up. She saw a boy, who was around her age, leaning over the adjacent metal fence.

"Are you alright?" he repeated.

"I...I'm fine," Meghan replied, trying to catch her breath after having the wind knocked out of her.

"Are you sure?" the boy inquired once again. "I saw you fall off the hammock – it looked pretty bad."

"I'm fine," Meghan snapped. *He must think I'm a complete klutz,* she thought with embarrassment.

"I'm glad you're okay," the boy smiled. "My name's Justin Grove. I saw your family moving in last week. How do you like your new house?"

"It's okay," Meghan lied, finally getting up from the ground. *I must've hit my legs pretty bad*, she realized as pain shot through them.

"Where did you come from?" Justin inquired, not noticing her discomfort.

"Far from here."

"Then this must be very different for you," he joked.

"Tell me about it," Meghan said with a small laugh.

"So, will you be going to Eastern Heights High in the fall?"

"Yes. It'll be my last year of high school." Meghan smiled, while thinking about the freedom she would have after graduating. Unknown to her parents, she planned to delay going to college and travel instead.

"Next year is my last also," Justin replied casually.

"That's nice," Meghan replied, not knowing what else to say. She felt as if the conversation would soon be coming to an abrupt end. To avoid an awkward silence, she gave Justin a polite smile, bid him goodbye and then headed into her house.

Meghan hurried to the refrigerator and put ice on her throbbing head. *I'll never sit on another hammock as long as I live*, she cringed.

* * *

"Hello neighbor! I see you're staying away from that hammock."

Meghan looked up from her chair to see Justin leaning over the fence. "Wouldn't *you*?" she replied.

"Probably," Justin said laughing. "Do you have any plans for today?" he asked quickly.

Meghan raised the novel in her hands and directed her eyes towards it. "Other than reading the latest Heather Beck book? No."

"Would you help me with something then?"

Meghan shot him a curious look but nodded anyway.

"You see," Justin began to explain, "the neighbor's cat came into my yard, climbed a tree and is now stuck up there."

"Why did the cat run up the tree in the first place?" Meghan wondered out loud.

"My dog chased him up there," Justin confessed.

"Why don't you just get a ladder and climb up there?"

"I'm afraid of heights."

Meghan made a display of playfully rolling her eyes. "What a man," she teased.

"You don't understand," Justin moaned, looking at her with pleading eyes. "The owner of the cat, Mrs. Hull, really dislikes me. She thinks my dog is a hazard to the public. She would go berserk if she found out her precious cat was stuck in my tree."

"Alright, I'm coming," Meghan said as she stood up and placed her book on the chair.

"Thanks," Justin said, while opening the gate that led to his yard.

Meghan helped Justin get a ladder from his garage and carry it to the tree. She looked up into the tall tree to see a frightened black cat clinging onto a branch.

"She looks really scared," Meghan commented as she began to climb the ladder.

"When you get the cat, make sure you hold her tight!" Justin called to Meghan. "Don't let her get away!"

Meghan reached the top of the ladder and then began to climb the branches. She winced as the maple tree's harsh bark scraped her hands. Meghan looked into the terrified green eyes of the cat, trying to forget about her own discomfort.

"It's alright, kitty," Meghan said soothingly as she reached for the cat. "Ouch!" she wailed as the cat lunged forward and scratched her.

Meow! the cat cried, right before moving swiftly down the tree without any difficulty.

"I thought you said that *thing* couldn't get down by itself!" Meghan yelled at Justin, not knowing if she was angrier at him or the cat.

Meghan pressed her hurt hand against her white t-shirt as she began climbing down the ladder. With every step she took, the ladder shook.

"Hold the ladder tighter!" Meghan called to Justin. When she received no reply, she turned her head to see that he was no longer there. *I can't believe he just left me here*, she panicked, realizing that she was seven feet off the ground.

Meghan used both hands to steady herself as she carefully made her way down the ladder. As she slid

4

her hands down the metal ladder, the hand which the cat had scratched scraped against a sharp corner. Meghan's hand instinctively shot backwards. She screamed as she felt herself falling off the ladder. Meghan lay on the ground and let out a quiet moan. She was filled with terror once again as the ladder began to fall towards her. She crossed her arms protectively over her face and waited to be crushed.

When nothing happened a few seconds later, she opened her eyes and saw Justin holding the ladder. She watched him fling it in the other direction and then hurry to her side.

"Are you okay?" he asked in a worried tone.

"No," Meghan snapped as she got up slowly. Her back, as well as her double cut hand, throbbed painfully. "Why did you leave me on the ladder like that?"

"I'm so sorry," Justin said sincerely. "Mrs. Hull's cat began to chase me after she'd climbed down the tree. I had to get away from her."

Meghan was flabbergasted at Justin's excuse. "The cat wouldn't have hurt you," she hissed, "because it left all its claws in me!" She shoved her bleeding finger towards Justin's face.

"I'll...I'll get you a bandage," he offered, while backing away in disgust.

"Don't bother," Meghan snapped as she walked through the gate.

Later in the afternoon, Meghan was still thinking about the incident at Justin's house. She wasn't only mad at Justin's behavior, but also disappointed. She'd thought he seemed like a nice guy who had the potential to become a great friend. But now that she

5

knew better, she never wanted to lay eyes on him again.

The ringing of the doorbell interrupted Meghan's thoughts.

"I'm painting my nails! Can you get the door?" Mrs. Bradford called to Meghan from the bedroom next door.

Meghan complained under her breath but got up anyway. When she opened the door, the person who she'd just been thinking of was standing there.

"What are you doing here?" Meghan snapped.

"I came to apologize and give you a peace offering," Justin said, smiling sweetly.

"Where's the peace offering?" Meghan retorted.

"Oh!" Justin exclaimed, as if remembering something. "It's in my backyard. It's too heavy for me to lift. Can you come and get it?"

"You want me to pick up my gift?" Meghan asked in astonishment. "You're unbelievable!"

"Please, Meghan. I really want you to have it."

"What makes you think I can lift it?"

"You look stronger than me," Justin said with a wink.

"Thanks, I think," Meghan said with a confused laugh. "Okay, I'll get it. What is it anyway?" she asked as she closed the door behind her and headed to Justin's house.

"You'll find out," he said mysteriously. "But before you do, I have something to confess."

"What is it now?" Meghan asked, annoyed at yet another disturbance in their friendship.

"I lied when I said I was afraid of heights. I'm actually afraid of cats. That's why I ran away when she came down the tree."

"Why didn't you just tell me that in the first place?" Meghan asked, rolling her eyes for the second time that day.

"It sounds better to be afraid of heights than a furry little cat," Justin confessed.

"You're forgiven," Meghan said. "But I'm never going to climb a ladder for you again. I don't care if it's you up there," she added, pointing to the tall maple tree. "You'll just have to stay there!"

Justin laughed and Meghan soon joined in.

"Here it is," Justin said abruptly as they stopped in the corner of his backyard.

"Excuse me?" Meghan asked, not sure if she'd heard him correctly.

"It's behind the leaves," Justin explained, sensing her confusion.

Meghan bent down and pushed the long, dark leaves away from the fence. Against the fence, in the very corner, was a large potted plant.

"That's the peace offering?" Meghan asked in confusion.

Justin nodded. "You like it, don't you?"

Meghan looked at the potted plant. The pot was a deep shade of red and had a high curve at the top to keep the soil from spilling over. The plant was like no other she'd ever seen. Although the soil was a healthy shade of dark brown, the trunk of the plant was a sickly color of yellow. Each branch held several green needles.

"It's definitely a different gift," Meghan finally answered. "What type of tree is it?"

"A pine tree," Justin answered in an uncomfortable tone of voice. "So, are you going to take it to your backyard?"

Meghan looked at Justin suspiciously. "Why are you so keen to get rid of such a unique plant? Does it have a disease that will kill all the other plants in my backyard?"

"No!" Justin exclaimed, trying to look and sound hurt. "I really like this plant, but I want you to have it."

"If you like it so much, why do you keep it behind another plant?"

"I didn't want anyone to steal it. You ask a lot of questions," Justin replied with a nervous laugh.

Meghan wasn't fully satisfied with Justin's answer but she took it as the truth anyway. She bent down and pried her fingers under the red pot.

"It is heavy," Meghan commented as she grunted out loud.

"Don't break it," Justin advised nervously.

"I won't," Meghan said with annoyance. "Ouch!" she said suddenly, letting the plant fall a few inches to the ground. The potted plant landed with a thump, but it didn't break.

"Did it jab you?" Justin asked, still using the same nervous tone.

"Yes," Meghan replied, holding tightly onto her finger.

"I jabbed myself on one of the needles before," he said solemnly.

"Well, thanks for the warning," she replied, picking up the plant again. "I should stay away from you. I always get hurt when we're together."

"I'm really sorry," Justin said in a sorrowful tone. "I'm very, very sorry."

As Meghan walked through the gate that he held open for her, she cast him a weird glance. "It's okay," she said, prolonging the word okay. "It doesn't hurt anymore."

"I know," Justin replied.

"Thanks for the plant," Meghan said as she placed it against the wall of her house.

Meghan had just turned her back to Justin for a second, but when she turned around again the gate was locked and he was nowhere to be seen. *He really is weird,* she thought as she headed into her house.

* * *

Meghan woke up in the middle of the night with a pain in her hand. At first she thought the pain was from the cat scratch or the cut from the ladder. She began to panic, thinking she'd contracted either rabies or blood poisoning. Meghan soon realized, however, that it was the other hand which was painful.

It's from the pine needle, Meghan thought.

In the dark, she hurried through her bedroom and the hallway until she came to the bathroom. She flicked on the light, looked at her finger and then gasped. Her index finger was red and swollen. It was double the size of what it used to be. At the tip of her finger where she'd been jabbed, was a small, dark green circle.

"Mom! Dad!" Meghan cried as she ran into her parent's bedroom.

"What's wrong?" Mr. Bradford asked, sitting upright in bed.

"I jabbed myself on a pine tree and now my finger is swollen and has a dark green mark!" Meghan was beginning to really panic. Her face flushed red and her heart raced.

"A pine tree?" Mrs. Bradford asked, finally sitting up. "How could you? We don't have any pine trees in our yard."

"It was a potted pine tree," Meghan answered. "I got it from the boy next door."

"I didn't know you had made a new friend. Is he nice?" Mr. Bradford inquired.

"He's just swell," Meghan said cheekily. "Now can we please concentrate on my infected finger?"

"You'll be fine," Mrs. Bradford said soothingly. "Why don't you have your father take a look at it?"

Mr. Bradford grumbled something about Meghan being a hypochondriac, but he got up anyway. He followed her to the bathroom where she showed him her finger.

"That is weird," Mr. Bradford admitted, upon studying her finger. "Was the plant sprayed with any chemicals?"

"I don't know," Meghan confessed.

"Do you feel alright apart from your sore finger? Do you have a fever?"

"I guess I'm okay," Meghan replied. "I just feel panicky about my finger."

"That's natural – for you anyway," Mr. Bradford said with an affectionate kiss on his daughter's head. "I'm sure you're fine. I'll take another look at your finger in the morning. If the swelling hasn't gone down, we can go see a doctor."

Meghan nodded, already feeling calmer. "Thanks," she said, heading back to her room.

"Sweet dreams," her father said.

* * *

Meghan woke up the next morning to find that her finger was no longer swollen or painful. She did, however, still have the unusual green mark.

"How's the finger?" Mr. Bradford asked as Meghan entered the kitchen.

"Fine, except for the green mark."

Mr. Bradford looked at the finger she offered him. "I really don't know what that is," he said, after a minute of examination.

"Well, I'm sure it'll go away just like the swelling and pain did," Meghan reasoned as she pulled her hand away. She was no longer concerned about her finger. She was too busy looking forward to spending the day in the backyard. "I'm going to eat outside," Meghan explained as she took her bowl of cereal and headed towards the sliding door.

"Meghan?" Mr. Bradford called her back.

"Yes?"

"Your mother and I will be leaving for her co-worker's wedding in about an hour. Will you be alright by yourself?"

"Of course," Meghan replied, astonished that her mother had made friends so quickly at her new job.

Seconds later, Meghan was soaking up the morning rays while chomping on some cold, sugary cereal. She spent most of the morning outside, feeling lonely without her parents or friends. In the quietness, Meghan's thoughts returned to her home and friends in the prairie. Her thoughts were suddenly interrupted by the sound of the neighbor's door opening. She looked up, hoping to see Justin. Instead, she saw someone who was presumably Justin's mother.

"Hello neighbor," Mrs. Grove said, upon seeing Meghan looking at her.

Like mother, like son, Meghan thought to herself with a secret smile. "Hi," she greeted, getting up to shake Mrs. Grove's hand.

After a few moments of general chit-chat, Meghan decided to inquire about Justin. "Is Justin home today?" she asked, hoping to find someone to hang out with.

"Justin," Mrs. Grove said wistfully, tears filling her eyes.

"Is everything okay?" Meghan asked, shocked at Mrs. Grove's emotional reaction.

"Oh, everything's fine now, but it wasn't two weeks ago." Mrs. Grove stopped talking to dab a tissue at the corner of her eyes.

"What happened?"

"He disappeared for a week."

"Excuse me?" Meghan choked. "He disappeared?"

"He just vanished. Then one day he showed up. He offered no explanation of his whereabouts. I was in such a frantic state! Did he say anything to you about where he went?"

"No. I didn't even know he'd been missing. He said nothing about it."

"Of course, you hadn't moved into your new house at that point. I was just hoping he'd talked to you."

Meghan shook her head and spread her hands towards Mrs. Grove, indicating that she knew nothing. Suddenly, Mrs. Grove grabbed Meghan's hand and stared at it in shock.

"No!" Mrs. Grove gasped.

"What?" Meghan demanded, trying to pull her hand away.

"You have the mark also," she said in a cold voice.

Meghan looked down to see the green mark, which had appeared after being jabbed by the pine needle. "What do you mean by also?"

"Justin had the same mark before he disappeared."

"No!" Meghan yelled. She pulled her arm away with such strength that Mrs. Grove lost her grip.

"Stay away from my family, especially Justin," Mrs. Grove threatened, before running into her house and locking the door.

Despite the hot summer weather, Meghan shivered. She looked up at Justin's house and saw the curtains at a window being drawn shut. *Did Justin just see what happened?* she wondered.

Meghan wasn't able to sleep well that night. Flashbacks from her conversation with Justin and especially Mrs. Grove kept running through her head. Her mind was also preoccupied with thoughts of the potted pine tree she'd been given.

He did seem very keen to get rid of it and I did develop the mark after being jabbed by the tree, Meghan thought. *Perhaps anyone who is jabbed by the tree disappears.* She couldn't suppress the urge to laugh out loud. *A tree that makes people disappear? Yeah right. Get a life, Meghan!*

Meghan grew serious as she began to think about her neighbors. *They're obviously not normal,* she thought. She cast a glance at her open window and got up to close it. Although she loved the breeze, she was too concerned about her neighbors to leave it open.

When Meghan reached the window, she stared at the Grove's house for a few minutes. All the windows appeared black and no one seemed to be awake. Relaxing a little, she leaned over to shut the window. Suddenly, she caught sight of a red light being projected onto her backyard deck. Her eyes searched the area, but she couldn't find the source of the light.

13

It looks as if it's coming from my house, Meghan finally realized with a shudder.

Too afraid to leave her room, Meghan leaned over the open window as far as she dared and looked down at the house. What she saw made her gasp. The red light was coming from the potted pine tree. She quickly pulled herself upward and stared at the Grove's house.

What kind of plant did Justin give me? Meghan wondered.

The red light was still coming from the potted plant, but now it was blinking. Instinctively, Meghan looked at her index finger. In the pale moonlight, she could see that the green mark on her finger had become bigger.

Meghan shut the window tightly, fastened the lock on her bedroom door and then proceeded to her bed to shake in fear.

Stop it, Meghan, she suddenly told herself. *Stop being afraid all the time.*

Meghan forced herself to stop shaking as she went to the window and opened it once again. Staring at the potted pine tree, she saw that all its needles were now flashing. She backed away from the window and tried to calm her racing heart.

What should I do? Meghan asked herself through deep breaths.

Meghan wished her parents would hurry back from the wedding. Unfortunately, they'd be at least another two hours since the venue was out of town.

I have to find out what's going on, Meghan decided as she quickly put on a pair of jeans and then rummaged through her closet. After finding a baseball bat, she unlocked her bedroom door and headed down the stairs.

14

In the darkness, Meghan tried to remember the whereabouts of the tables and staircase as she maneuvered through the house. Her memory failed her as she took a step forward and felt nothing but air underneath her foot. Meghan made a desperate attempt to grab for the banister, but she didn't have enough time. She felt her body in freefall before she landed at the bottom of the staircase. The baseball bat flew from her hands and tumbled down after her.

"Ouch," Meghan moaned in pain. She lay at the bottom of the staircase for a moment, afraid to move her body just in case anything was broken. Although her side ached, she hadn't broken any bones.

Ding Dong.

Meghan's whole body tensed at the sound of the doorbell. She knew her parents had a key and that they would never ring the doorbell. Meghan looked at the door, wondering who was behind it.

Ding Dong. Ding Dong.

Meghan's heart began to beat faster.

Ding Dong. Ding Dong. Ding Dong.

The blood in Meghan's veins ran cold as she listened to the persistent ringing of the doorbell. She had no idea who was behind the door. The Bradfords didn't know anyone here, except Mrs. Bradfords' co-workers who'd all be at the wedding right now. Meghan also knew the weird and unpredictable Groves. Suddenly, a new sound came from the door.

Meghan slowly got up and went towards the door. She had no intention of opening it; she just wanted to test her theory on the cause of the new noise. Shakily, Meghan placed her hand upon the door handle. Her heart missed a beat as she felt it move under her fingers.

It's trying to break in, Meghan thought in a panic, not knowing what "it" was. Her breath came in shallow rasps as she stood on her tip-toes and peered through the peep-hole in the door. Two flashing red lights greeted her.

"No!" Meghan screamed in fear as well as frustration. She began to pound on the door with both fists. "Leave me alone!" she cried. "Whoever you are, leave me alone!"

In reply to her shouts of protest, the person behind the door began to pound back. The pounding continued, getting fiercer as the seconds ticked by. The door began to rattle and then the lock broke.

Meghan spun around and ran quickly down the basement stairs. The old wooden stairs creaked beneath her. She'd just reached the basement when a loud crash echoed from upstairs. Whatever was behind the door was now in the house.

Meghan had run down to the basement because there was a large window in which she could escape. Her only concern now was getting out of the house before the thing got to her.

The window was easy to see against the pale moonlight. Meghan unlocked the window and pulled it open. She knew she didn't have time to be quiet as she pulled a small black handle on the screen and ripped it open. Meghan jumped through the open window and pulled herself onto the damp grass. She was almost completely on the grass when a pair of cold hands grabbed her ankles.

"No!" Meghan cried, kicking her feet until the person let go. Unable to resist the urge of knowing who had broken into her house, she looked behind her. "Justin!" she exclaimed.

"Hello, Meghan," Justin said in a subdued voice. His glowing red eyes stared into Meghan's, as if trying to hypnotize her.

Meghan backed away from Justin as he crawled out of the basement window. She began to run but had only taken a few steps when she found herself amongst an array of red lights. The lights, which came from the potted plant, pulsated and grew larger. They grew into long beams and encompassed Meghan.

Breaking out of the spell which the brilliant lights cast upon her, Meghan attempted to run once more. She bumped into the beams, unable to break through them.

If I can't get past the light beams, maybe Justin can't get through them, Meghan thought. She peered through the beams in search of Justin. He'd disappeared as quickly as he had appeared.

Meghan had just started to relax a little when she felt someone tap her shoulder. She turned around slowly, not wanting to see who was behind her.

"Your turn," Justin said in an almost sad tone.

"Go away!" Meghan shouted in terror. "Just go away!"

"You're the one who will be going away," Justin replied in the same sad voice. "I'm sorry, but it was the only way I could save myself. I wish you the best of luck so that you may return in a week. I'll watch and wait for you," he promised.

"Wait! Tell me what you mean!" Meghan demanded as she watched Justin vanish behind the light beams.

Meghan pushed against the light beams. They resisted her efforts and grew larger and brighter in response. Her eyes ached in the brightness. Meghan let out a defeated whimper as she saw the light beams closing in on her. She said a prayer as she felt them sweep over her body.

Meghan's eyes fluttered open. She lay on her back, shivering from the late night dew that covered the grass. Darkness surrounded her, but with the passing of a cloud, the moonlight allowed her to see large pine needles above her head.

"Huh?" Meghan exclaimed out loud, sitting up quickly. She strained her neck and stared up at the pine needles which hovered over her head. *No, they're not hovering,* Meghan realized. As she looked to her side, she noticed familiar-looking yellow branches and a trunk.

Meghan slowly got to her feet and walked towards the trunk. She ran her hand over the sickly-looking bark. It wasn't rough and sturdy, like she thought it would be. Instead, it was mushy and smelled like decaying eggs. Disgusted, Meghan wiped her hands on the grass. A pungent smell now came from her hands. However, it didn't smell the same as the bark. Meghan raised her hands to her face and gagged in response. She hadn't noticed earlier but the dew also smelled horrible.

"What is this place?" Meghan muttered. She took a few steps forward and then she began to run. She had to get to the end of the garden or, in her wildest fears, the edge of the pot.

Meghan left the slippery grass and trekked upon rich, dark soil. She could no longer ignore the alarm-bells which were going off in her head.

I'm in the potted plant, Meghan thought in a panic. *How could this happen? I must be dreaming.*

Meghan was so wrapped up in her thoughts that she didn't notice she'd neared the edge of the pot. A shrill scream escaped from her mouth as she tripped over the edge and began to fall.

Meghan experienced whiplash as a large net caught her and sent her flying upwards. She shook from the near death experience as she was lifted up. As Meghan was pulled back into the pot, she came face-to-face with four little evil-looking men. She let out a scream and struggled to free herself from the net.

"She's a silly one," said one of the little men.

Hearing the man's voice made Meghan silent. He spoke in a squeaky tone that would either make you laugh or wince and cover your ears. Meghan stared at the four men from behind the netting. They were shorter than her and had unusually large heads. Their eyes were so big and black that she was unable to tell where the pupil ended and where the iris began.

Maybe they don't even have pupils, Meghan thought with a shudder.

The men were chubby and dressed in a robe-like outfit which was split in half by the color red and green. Although they wore the traditional colors of Christmas, they looked anything but jolly. Their glossy black hair made them look very evil.

"You're right," another man replied. "First she jumps out of the pot and then she struggles to escape from the net which saved her life."

The four men laughed hysterically. Their laugh sounded like a dozen screeching owls.

"Who are you?" Meghan cried, unable to control her frustration and confusion any longer.

"We're gnomes," one of the gnomes, who hadn't spoken yet, replied, "and soon you'll be one too!"

Meghan stared at the gnomes with a blank expression and then laughed. *What a weird dream,* she thought. *I'll play along and see what happens next.* "Will you please let me out?" she asked kindly.

The gnomes looked at each other in surprise.

"She's not screaming or crying like the others," one of the gnomes observed.

"We'll let you go if you promise not to jump over the pot again," another gnome bargained.

"I promise I won't jump," Meghan answered truthfully.

The gnomes looked at each other and nodded in unison. They worked together until she was free.

Meghan's neck felt sore from the whiplash, but she blamed it on the way her body must be sleeping.

"My name is Meghan," she said, offering her hand to each gnome.

"I'm Nonie," the first gnome said. Nonie's hand was short and very difficult to shake.

Meghan shook the three remaining gnomes' hands, learning their names along the way. "Konie, Monie, Donie and Nonie," she repeated out loud. "What unusual names!"

"Would you like to know why you're here?" Nonie asked, confused by her calm demeanor.

"Sure," Meghan replied with an amused smile, still believing she was dreaming.

"I'll start at the beginning," Nonie said. "You're in the Garden Gnome's Pot. It's where Konie, Monie, Donie and I have called home our whole lives. A few months ago, the Garden Gnome's Pot was sprayed with a chemical. The chemical killed many of the gnomes and horribly affected the delicate environment of the pot. After we were sprayed, our pine tree deteriorated."

"And then things started to get really weird," Konie interrupted with an almost evil grin.

"The owner of the pot jabbed himself on a pine needle," Nonie continued. "The blood from his finger supplied our tree with energy and it began to grow again. The next thing we knew, our owner had shrunk to our size and joined us in the pot. After conducting careful scientific research, the other gnomes and I realized that when he jabbed himself blood was transferred. Our owner not only gave us blood but we gave him our blood as well. He was injected by a gnome genome. This explained his new size and presence in the pot. We soon figured out that we could only survive through human DNA. As the days passed, our owner began to grow back into his normal size. When we saw this happening, we tested our hypothesis and confirmed that by injecting him with our genome our environment thrived and he became small once again."

"That's terrible!" Meghan interjected.

"We didn't think it was fair to keep him with us forever," Nonie replied defensively. "We wanted to give him a chance to escape. After careful consideration, we decided to let our DNA disintegrate in his body, but only if he passed three games."

"And if he didn't pass?" Meghan asked curiously.

Nonie chuckled evilly. "Our owner passed all the games so we didn't put any more of our genome into him," he explained, not answering Meghan's question. "However, before he left we put a spell on him. It ensured that he'd find us new blood. The spell worked and soon a nice young man named Justin Grove came and played with us. He also passed the games. We let him go and now it's your turn." Nonie stopped talking and took a deep breath. He looked at Meghan, waiting for her reaction.

"Whoa," Meghan said with a smile. "I have some imagination! This is definitely the most interesting dream I've had in a while."

"It's not a dream. It's real. We're real. And you're really here."

"Uh huh," Meghan said with a mocking smile, while reaching out to pinch the gnome's face. "Aren't you a weird little thing?" she said, as if talking to a baby. The gnome's skin felt soft and blubbery between her fingers.

All of a sudden, Nonie hissed and then bit Meghan. His long, black teeth scraped her skin, making her bleed.

Meghan looked down at her hand in shock. "That hurt," she said in a cold realization. "This...this is real. It's really happening."

"Shall we start the games?" Nonie said with a little smile that wasn't completely innocent.

"Okay," Meghan whispered. "I'll play."

"A wise decision," Nonie said, nodding with approval. "I hope all your decisions are as wise because if they're not, you'll be staying here for an awfully long time."

"I'm not going to lose," Meghan said forcefully, realizing the severity of the situation. "What's the first game?"

The gnomes led Meghan back to the tree. Konie scurried away and returned a minute later with several pine needles. The pine needles were different colors consisting of green, yellow, purple and blue. They were bundled together with a piece of rope. Meghan watched as Konie untied the pine needles and let them fall to the ground. She noticed that one of the pine needles was black.

"The game is called Pick Up The Pine Needles," Konie explained. "The purpose is to pick up the

22

pine needles very carefully. You may only keep the pine needles which don't move any of the other pine needles. Each pine needle has a point system. The blue pine needle is worth 20 points, the purple 15, the yellow 10, and the green 5."

"What about the black?" Meghan asked, interrupting the gnome.

"Whoever moves the black pine needle must forfeit the needle they intended to pick up and take the black one instead. If the black pine needle is kept to the end, the player whose turn it is must pick it up. Whoever possesses the black pine needle will lose 100 points. The winner of the game is the person – or gnome," Konie added with a giggle, "who has the most points."

"Wait a minute," Meghan interjected. "My chances of winning are only one in four."

"We realize that," Konie said. "That's why only one of us will play against you. You may take your pick, Meghan."

Meghan looked at the gnomes and examined their fingers. She wanted to play against the gnome who had the least dainty fingers. Meghan thought Monie's hands looked a bit bigger than the others.

"I'll play against Monie," she said confidently.

Monie looked at the other gnomes. They all sighed in disappointment.

"Another wise choice," Nonie said.

"Let's begin," Monie said. "You may go first."

Meghan walked around the pile of small colorful pine needles. She began to reach for an accessible purple needle.

"Wait!" Monie shouted suddenly. "In the excitement we forgot to pick the High Spectator."

"The what?" Meghan asked in confusion, a bit upset by the interruption.

23

"The High Spectator," Monie explained. "That's the gnome who watches the game from above. He'll be able to get a better view of what's happening."

"I'll go," Donie volunteered, scrambling up the tree and placing himself on a branch.

Meghan jumped back as a large yellow liquid drop fell from the branch that Donie was sitting on. The gnomes looked at each other with concern.

"Hold on just a minute," Meghan said, while staring at the yellow gooey mess. "How can I trust you to call the plays truthfully?"

"We have an oath," Monie replied. "Humans may think gnomes are devious, but that isn't true. We always keep our promises and play fair."

"Let the game begin!" Donie called from above.

Meghan took a deep breath and reached for the purple pine needle. She winced as the needle slightly bumped a yellow one. She continued on, hoping that Donie hadn't noticed.

"Foul!" Donie's squeaky voice rang out happily.

Meghan's chest tightened in fear. She couldn't believe the game had got off to such a bad start.

Monie took his turn and successfully retrieved the yellow needle which Meghan had bumped.

"Monie: ten! Meghan: zero!" Donie called out loud.

Meghan examined the pile of needles and chose a purple one that lay near the edge. Ever so carefully, she pushed the purple needle against the grass and slid it out. "Yes!" she cried, after retrieving it successfully. "Meghan: fifteen! Monie: ten!" she called up proudly to Donie, who pouted his large pink lips.

"The game isn't over yet," Konie spoke from the sidelines.

Monie stepped closer to the pile of pine needles and examined them for a few minutes.

"Hurry up," Meghan said impatiently.

"Shhh!" Monie scolded, casting Meghan an angry glance. He bent down to retrieve a blue needle.

"It touched another needle!" Meghan shouted triumphantly.

Monie grunted as Meghan easily retrieved the blue needle he'd left.

"That's thirty points for me," Meghan said happily. "How much do you have?" she mocked Monie.

Monie cast another glare at Meghan and then reached for a green needle. He retrieved it successfully and then poked her in the face with it.

"Ouch!" Meghan cried, rubbing her hurt cheek. "Did you just take more DNA from me?"

The gnomes all laughed.

"Of course not," Monie said in between high pitch giggles. "The pieces in Pick Up The Pine Needles are fake. Don't you know anything?"

"When it comes to this weird place? No," Meghan admitted.

"On with the game!" Donie shouted from the tree branch. "And do hurry up – I don't know how much longer this branch can hold me."

Meghan looked up to see the branch dripping more yellow liquid. She almost felt sorry for the gnomes and the decaying plant in which they lived.

She forced back all sympathy and reached for a blue needle. Very carefully, she slid the needle from the pile. Meghan let out a sigh of relief as she successfully retrieved the blue needle without disturbing any other needles. She now had fifty points.

The game continued for another half an hour. Meghan was doing well at one hundred and sixty five points. She was using the strategy of only aiming for the blue and purple needles. The problem with the strategy was that there were less blue and purple needles than yellow and green. Since there were less, the blue and purple needles were more likely to be under other needles, which made them harder to retrieve. Monie was also doing well at one hundred and forty five points. His strategy was to go for the easier to retrieve, but of less worth, yellow and green needles.

As the game neared the end, only four pine needles remained – two greens, a yellow and the dreaded black.

Meghan's heart was racing. It was her turn, but she didn't know what move to make. All the needles were overlapping. The needle that would be the easiest to retrieve was the yellow one. If she picked it, Monie would choose a green one. From watching his ability throughout the game, Meghan didn't think he was capable of getting it. If he didn't retrieve a green pine needle, Meghan would take it. Then Monie would easily get the last green one and she would be stuck with the black needle.

Not really sure if her plan was smart or not, Meghan went for the yellow needle and purposely made it touch the green one.

"Foul!" Donie cried.

Monie looked at Meghan suspiciously but went for the yellow needle anyway. He obtained it without any difficulty.

"Meghan has one hundred and sixty five points! Monie has one hundred and fifty five points!" Donie shouted down from the tree.

Meghan went for the green needle, bringing it out and then taping it against the other green needle.

"Foul!" Donie shouted once again.

Monie went for the green needle which Meghan had left in a convenient position. He retrieved it successfully.

"Meghan: one hundred and sixty five! Monie: one hundred and sixty!" Donie called.

Meghan took a deep breath and tried to sooth her nerves. This was one needle she really wanted to have. The end of the green needle was touching the black one. Trying to control her hands that were shaking slightly, she lowered them and gently slid her fingers along the green needle. She pulled it slowly until it was far away from the black needle. Meghan held the green needle in her hand and sighed. She couldn't believe she'd just played a game upon which her freedom depended.

Monie took the black needle and grunted.

"Final score!" Donie called, "Meghan: one hundred and seventy! Monie: fifty five!" Donie climbed down the tree quickly and congratulated Meghan. "Good work. You played well. However, you chose to play against Monie – our worst player. Now that you've played with him, you can't pick him again. I must warn you that our games get harder as they go on."

"What game is next?" Meghan asked, trying to hide the fear that Donie had just instilled in her.

"No more games for today," Nonie said grumpily. "Tonight, we eat and rest. We'll play tomorrow."

"Sounds fine to me," Meghan muttered, relaxing just a little.

* * *

Meghan woke up the next morning, wondering where she was. It didn't take long for the events of yesterday to come flooding back to her. At first she thought it was a dream, but the scratchy blanket, which was made from intertwined pine needles, made her realize that this was really happening.

Flinging the blanket off, Meghan walked towards the gnomes. They slept upright and looked like they were made from plastic. They were like the gnomes one would find in a garden, but she knew better.

Meghan touched Nonie, surprised at the heat which was generated from the plastic-looking body. As she reached to touch Nonie's face, he grabbed her hand. She jumped backwards and let out a scream.

Nonie laughed. His laughter awoke the other gnomes, who stretched and then headed to the tree trunk.

"Hey, where are you going?" Meghan yelled, running after the gnomes.

"To get breakfast," Donie replied.

"But last night we nibbled on pine needles," Meghan protested.

"Yes," Konie replied. "But that was dinner. For breakfast we have sap."

"Sap?" Meghan repeated, pursing her lips at the thought of licking anything that came from the decaying tree.

Nonie brushed aside some pine needles and revealed a tap at the base of the tree. He took five bowls, which were made from intertwining pine needles, and turned on the tap. At first crystal clear sap poured from the tap, but soon yellowish goo took its place. Nonie sighed. He'd only filled two bowls when he turned off the tap.

"This always happens," Nonie explained as he handed one bowl to Meghan and the other to Donie. "As you've probably figured out, we'll die if we don't get the genome of other living creatures."

"Why don't you gather the genome from animals?" Meghan asked, while sucking the sap. It tasted surprisingly good.

"It would be too hard to get an animal to jab itself on our needles. Obviously, it's easier for us to communicate with humans. Besides, our potted plant can only survive on the human DNA structure."

"This is too weird," Meghan muttered as she watched Nonie turn on the tap again.

"Maybe," Nonie replied, "but it's all we know."

"It's time for another game," Nonie announced, after everyone had finished their morning sap.

"Is this necessary?" Meghan began to plead, not wanting to risk her freedom once again.

"It's your only option," Nonie said sadly. "I'm sorry. I really don't want to take you away from your family and friends, but if we want to survive it has to be this way."

Meghan suddenly thought about her family. She wondered if gnome time was the same as human time. Meghan shook her head sadly, thinking about her worried parents searching for her when the whole time she was, ironically, in the potted plant that leaned against the wall of their house. These thoughts made her sadness turn into anger.

"Why did you make Justin target me?" Meghan demanded hotly, remembering Justin's look of remorse when giving her the plant.

"We did no such thing!" Konie replied in a hurt tone. "A human who wins all three games is freed and then must get another human to touch a pine needle. However, we don't tell the human who to choose. That's their responsibility."

"Thanks, Justin," Meghan muttered angrily under her breath. "What's the next game?"

"Build A Tower," Monie replied.

"Excuse me?" Meghan asked with a racing heart. She knew she didn't have the skills to build a tower.

"Build A Tower," Monie repeated. "Each player uses pine needles to build a tower. The rules of this game are few and simple. You may build the tower any way you want. The player who builds the highest tower wins. If one of the players' tower falls, that player is automatically disqualified. Oh, and another thing," Monie added. "There's no time limit. The game continues until a tower falls."

"What size will the pine needles be?" Meghan inquired.

"The large size," Monie replied, "the size that's on the tree."

"You will climb the tree as you build," Konie added, upon seeing Meghan's confusion.

"Well," Meghan began, "what are we waiting for? Let's get started!"

Once all the pine needles were collected, the game began with Monie whistling between his two index fingers.

Before the game started, Meghan had examined the pine needles carefully and created a plan. She drove four pine needles into the ground, leaving just a few millimeters in between each needle. Meghan then placed a single needle on the ground and measured the length. With this measurement, she drove in four more needles. She began placing the needles on top of the side structures, making sure that each needle was snuggly between two others. She continued to build, making her tower as sturdy as possible.

Meghan was now climbing up the soft yellow tree, while dragging a dozen pine needles with her. She was working on an almost empty stomach and sweat was beginning to form on her forehead. She glanced at Konie, whom she'd picked as her competitor. He was building fast, but not quite as fast as her.

Meghan turned her head from Konie's direction and concentrated on building her own tower. Her back ached and her legs were tired, but she kept on going. She'd just started her seventeenth layer when she heard a loud crash and screams.

Meghan looked down from her tree branch to see Konie lying on top of his now disassembled tower. She scrambled down the tree and to the gnomes.

"What happened?" Meghan asked.

"The branch he was sitting on broke," Monie explained.

"Is he alright?"

Monie nodded in relief. "He has a bad sprain, but he'll be fine. Right, Konie?" he asked with a comforting smile.

"Yes," Konie replied quietly. "It hurts, but I'll be okay."

Meghan watched as Nonie helped Monie make a leg brace out of pine needles.

"Congratulations," Donie said suddenly to Meghan. "You've won your second game."

Meghan tried to hide her smile, but was unsuccessful in doing so. "Thanks," she replied as modestly as she could.

That night Meghan tossed and turned under her woven pine needle blanket. Images of her mother and father kept running through her mind. She thought about how worried they must be. She was also worried about the tall tales Mrs. Grove would be telling her parents.

"Can't sleep?" Nonie asked, seemingly appearing out of nowhere.

"No," Meghan sighed as she sat up. She always experienced mixed emotions around the gnomes. On the one hand, she felt sorry for them. However, they were also the reason she was stuck here in the first place. *Well, Justin gets some of the blame too,* she thought with loathing.

"How do you feel?" Nonie asked, sitting down beside her.

"Do you even care?" Meghan retorted, while moving away slightly.

"Yes," Nonie said quietly. "I like humans and I feel guilty about what we do to them."

"Oh, boo hoo," Meghan mocked. "Do you actually expect me to feel sorry for you?" Silence followed her question. "Well, I don't," she lied. "How did this weird place come into existence anyway?"

"How does anything come into existence? I don't have the answer to that question. I can only have faith that my world was created by the will of a higher power."

Meghan shot Nonie a half smile. "We're not that different. It's too bad we have to be on opposite sides."

"Yes, it is," Nonie agreed. "Get some sleep."

Meghan watched the gnome walk away. *Things keep on getting weirder,* she thought, before giving into the temptation of sleep.

* * *

Meghan awoke to a sweet smell the next morning. Her eyelids fluttered open to see Monie waving a bowl of sap in front of her face. When Monie realized he'd wakened her, he laughed in a high pitch tone.

That's one sound I don't want to wake up to everyday, Meghan thought. "Thanks," she said, taking the bowl of sap from Monie. She drank it without enjoying its sweetness; she was too anxious about today's game to enjoy anything.

"It's time to play," Nonie announced, after Meghan and the other gnomes had finished their bowls of sap.

Meghan was surprised to find herself feeling hurt by Nonie's announcement. Trying to ignore the emotion, she stepped forward. "Yes," she replied in a strong voice, "let's begin." She was determined not to let Nonie sense her fear.

"Today's game is called Flag Hunt. The objective is to find the green flag which Monie has hidden in the tree. The only rule is that there are no rules. The players may use any force they deem necessary to win. Whoever reaches the flag first wins."

"Alright," Meghan said, absorbing the information Nonie had just given her. "Let's get this game started. I'll play against Donie."

Nonie spoke before Donie had a chance to say anything. "I'm flattered you consider me worthy enough competition to avoid. However, the rules of our land clearly state that one of the gnomes, who plays against the human, must be me."

"You didn't tell me that," Meghan said, looking suspiciously at Nonie. "How was I supposed to know?"

"Well, you know now," Nonie said defensively. "Let's play."

Meghan approached the tree with Nonie. She looked up, searching for the flag.

Amused, Nonie snorted. "I can guarantee that you won't find the flag simply by looking up at the tree. It'll be well hidden."

"I bet you already know where it is. Monie probably told you where he hid it." Meghan secretly hoped her words would hurt Nonie. By the expression on his face, she was sure they had.

"Go!" Monie yelled suddenly.

Monie's call startled Meghan and left her a few moves behind Nonie. She quickly regained her bearings and scrambled up the tree. Meghan decided that it would be in her best interest to follow Nonie, just in case Monie had told him the location of the flag.

Meghan climbed the tree with difficulty. The branches felt damp; they made a sucking noise whenever she placed or removed her hands. Strategically, she made her way over to the cluster of pine needles which Nonie was furiously searching through. She positioned herself on a branch under Nonie and began searching. She was about to look in a nearby cluster when Nonie kicked her in the ribs.

"Ouch," Meghan moaned at the sudden pain. She let go of the branch and reached to comfort her throbbing side. When she felt herself slip from the branch, she grabbed the end of the branch on which Nonie was sitting. She watched in horror as he lifted his fist in the air and prepared to hit her hand. She quickly moved her hand and scurried to the trunk of the tree. She was afraid that the flag was indeed hidden there. At least that would explain Nonie's uncharacteristic behavior. When Meghan saw Nonie leaving that side of the tree, she quickly dismissed the thought. Instead, she began to climb higher.

Meghan searched through clusters of pine needles. She felt as if she'd been searching for hours, yet there were still many unchecked branches. Meghan began to fear that Nonie would find the flag and she'd be doomed to spend the rest of her life in a potted plant. She looked up to see that the tree was getting thinner.

I'm near the top, Meghan realized, shivering at the thought of being so high off the ground. She continued to look up at the tree. She was devoid of any hope as she thought about her family and friends.

When a strong wind blew, Meghan noticed something fluttering at the top of the tree. She raised her body and narrowed her eyes, trying to get a better look at the object. She gasped when she realized that it was the green flag.

Meghan's gasp alerted Nonie, who was less than eight feet away from her. She looked at him, praying that he hadn't seen what she had. The twinkle in Nonie's eyes indicated that he'd also noticed the flag. With a swift jump, Nonie began to race towards the top of the tree.

Oh no you don't, Meghan thought with determination as she sped after Nonie. Her legs ached and her breath came in shallow puffs, but she didn't care. Meghan climbed swiftly up the tree. She had soon passed Nonie and was just about to reach for the flag when he bit her. Meghan felt his teeth penetrate her skin, but she kept on stretching. She stretched until she had the flag firmly in her hands.

"Not again," Nonie muttered in disappointment. "You won fair and square," he commented. "Now it's time for you to go home."

A smile appeared on Meghan's face but it disappeared as quickly as it had come as Nonie reached out and pushed her off the branch.

Meghan's eyes fluttered open. She saw a dark sky above her head. She sat up, fearing that she was still in the potted plant. However, what she saw made her smile. She was lying on the deck; beside her was the potted plant. She was no longer in the plant nor was she the size of a gnome. She kneeled close to the potted plant and searched for the gnomes. She couldn't see them but she didn't dare touch the needles in a more thorough search.

"Meghan, you made it back! I'm so glad you're okay."

Meghan was so deep in thought that the noise frightened her. She jumped forward and reached her hand out to steady herself. In doing so, her hand pressed against the red pot. Her index finger touched a pine needle. She felt the needle slowly pierce her skin. Meghan stared at her finger in terror and then turned around to see who'd made her jab herself once again. Her stomach churned when she saw a guilty-looking Justin standing in the light of the moon.

"I wish I'd never met you," she said through clenched teeth.

* * *

A Weird Twist Of Fate

Knock, knock, knock.

"I'm getting dressed!" nineteen-year-old Judith called to the person who was knocking on her bedroom door.

"Alright, Miss Forge," Judith's housekeeper, Marion, said from behind the door. "But please hurry. The guests have started to arrive and your parents want you in the dining-room immediately."

"I'll be there in a minute," Judith said through a sigh.

Judith hated the fancy dinner parties her parents always dragged her to. Tonight, Mr. and Mrs. Forge were hosting a party at their house. Throughout the years, Judith's parents had spent endless hours telling her that she must always dress and behave properly. Judith acted like the young lady her parents wanted her to be. Unfortunately, that wasn't the person Judith wanted to be. Judith was a Goth, but that choice of lifestyle clashed with her parents. Mr. and Mrs. Forge had old-fashioned values, were very posh and thrived at formal occasions. Even though Judith wanted to wear an edgy black dress to dinner parties, she'd always worn the respectable ones her mother insisted on – until now.

Judith's heart raced with excitement as she looked into the full-length mirror and saw the epitome of a witch staring back at her. She was wearing a tight, long black dress that had red lace around the waist. The outfit was completed with the black lipstick, eye shadow and heavy eyeliner that covered her pale face. Her long, straight black hair swung over her shoulders as she turned away from the mirror and headed out of her bedroom.

Judith was anxious to get her big entrance over with. She knew her parents wouldn't be impressed. In fact, they would probably ground her for life. Normally, Judith wouldn't violate their wishes. However, she couldn't hide who she really was anymore. She wanted her parents and their friends to accept the real her. Judith was sure her parents would respect *her* wishes when they saw how important being a Goth was to her.

Judith could hear adults talking and wine glasses being clinked as they greeted each other. She took a deep breath and then entered the beautifully decorated dining-room.

At first no one seemed to notice her. They were all too busy bragging about their wonderful careers and children. Judith began to have second thoughts about her debut when she saw her parents talking to Mr. and Mrs. Patterson. The Pattersons were highly respected in the community due to their extensive work with charities. They'd also established the Helping Hands Charity which assisted low income families and the unemployed.

Judith was about to turn around, run back to her bedroom and change into a traditional light pink dress, but her eyes met Mrs. Patterson's before she had the chance to run away. She watched in fear as Mrs. Patterson's eyes went wide with surprise.

"Who is that?" Judith heard Mrs. Patterson ask Mrs. Forge.

"I guess this wasn't such a good idea after all," Judith muttered as Mrs. Forge turned around and stared at her daughter in shock.

"Mom, I can explain," Judith said, backing away as her mother marched towards her.

Mrs. Forge was silent as she grabbed her daughter's arm tightly and led her into the next room. She closed the door between the two rooms before she began to yell.

"Judith Hyacinth Forge! What do you think you're doing?"

"I...I just wanted to show everyone my true colors," Judith stuttered.

"Black isn't a color, it's a tint," Mrs. Forge seethed. "How dare you show up to my party like this. You know the rules and you deliberately disobeyed them. You've disappointed your father and me deeply. Oh, and the Pattersons! What will they think of our family now?"

Judith felt her blood boil in anger. "Don't you care about my thoughts and feelings? I'm sick of having to go to all these fancy dinner parties while pretending to be someone I'm not." She blinked furiously as she tried to keep her emotions under control. "Look at me, Mother," she said sadly. "This is who I truly am."

Mrs. Forge's face tightened in anger. "Go to your room and stay there for the rest of the night. I can't bear to look at you for a second longer while you're wearing that silly Halloween costume."

Sadness swept over Judith as Mrs. Forge exited the room, shutting her out in the process. She didn't try to hide the tears as she pressed her ear against the door and listened to her mother's conversation with Mrs. Patterson.

"That wasn't Judith, was it?" Mrs. Patterson asked in surprise.

"Yes, it was," Mrs. Forge said with fake enthusiasm. "Judith's playing a witch in a community theater production. Our daughter is really interested in drama. She wanted to give our guests a preview, but I told her she simply couldn't. I wouldn't want the play's coordinator to be upset about their finest talent demonstrating her gift before opening night."

Judith's mouth dropped open. *I can't believe my own mother is denying the true me!*

"Drama? Oh, you must be so proud of Judith," Mrs. Patterson said in relief.

"I am," Mrs. Forge replied with false pride.

Judith couldn't stand to hear any more lies. Hot tears saturated her face as she ran to her bedroom and flung herself onto her bed.

* * *

The warmth from the sun that shone through the window woke Judith up the following morning. She sat up slowly, wondering why her eyes felt so funny. Judith got the answer to her question when she looked down and saw that she was wearing a tight black dress. She sighed deeply as the events of last night returned to her mind.

Judith got up from bed and stretched. She realized that she'd fallen asleep crying and hadn't changed into her pajamas or brushed her teeth. However, Judith knew she had more important things to worry about.

A gentle knocking on the door startled Judith out of her thoughts.

I hope that's Mother with an apology, Judith thought. "Come in!" she called. Her heart sank as Marion walked into her room. *I should've known better than to expect an apology from my mother. I bet she wants an apology from me. Well, that's certainly not going to happen. I have a right to be who I want to be.*

"Are you feeling alright?" Marion asked in concern.

"I suppose so," Judith replied, not knowing what else to say.

"Aren't you going to get washed?" Marion asked, while looking at the black make-up that covered Judith's face as well as her white pillow.

"I just woke up," Judith explained.

Marion nodded in understanding. "Breakfast was served quite some time ago, but I can make something for you."

Judith shook her head. "It's alright. I think I'll go over to Samantha's house and grab something to eat at a coffee shop." She stopped talking when she saw Marion shifting uncomfortably. "What is it?" Judith asked, knowing that the housekeeper's discomfort was most likely caused by her mother. She always hated how demanding her mother was to Marion and the other previous live-in housekeepers.

"Mrs. Forge said she wanted you to clean the attic and gather any items that can be given to the Helping Hands Charity," Marion explained.

Judith couldn't believe her ears. She knew her mother was only making her do this to save face with the Pattersons.

"And once you're done," Marion continued with a red face, "your mother would like you to drop the items off at Mr. and Mrs. Patterson's house."

"I wonder why?" Judith asked rhetorically as she seethed out loud.

After a purposely prolonged breakfast, Judith trudged towards the attic. She didn't want to think about all the dust that would cling to her black top and jeans once she was inside the attic.

Judith had lived in the same four-story house her whole life. Her parents continuously bragged about how the house had been in the family for generations. Judith's distant ancestors had cleared the once heavily forested area and built the house there. At first it was just a small house, but over the years many additions were made to it, thus making it into the magnificent house that it was today. As her parents had reminded her countless times, the house was valued at over one million dollars.

Judith entered the storage room where the door to the attic was located. She slowly maneuvered through the pile of antique furniture and odds and ends that were no longer being used. She pulled on a thick brown rope to release the stairs that led to the attic.

Slowly and carefully, Judith made her way up the rickety old stairs. A smile played upon her lips as she thought about how bad her mother would feel if anything happened to her while she was cleaning the attic.

As Judith proceeded to climb the stairs, she was met with complete darkness. She felt an inch of dust as her hands clutched the attic floor. She moaned in disgust as she stepped inside. The air was so hot that she couldn't breathe. Every time she moved her feet, more dust was released into the air.

Judith reached for the small flashlight, which she'd put in her pocket, and then shone the beam in front of her. She let out a small gasp as she realized she wasn't alone. Three tall women were standing at the other end of the attic.

"What are you doing up here?" Judith yelled, trying to frighten the intruders. Her heart raced as she waited for a reply. "How did you get up here?" she demanded once again.

The three women stood still and refused to talk.

Judith swallowed hard as she approached the women. She clutched her flashlight and shone it on a woman's face. She screamed in horror when she saw that the lady had no face.

Judith turned around and ran as fast as she could. She knew she had to get out of the attic and find help. *Who will ever believe that there are three faceless women in our attic?* Judith thought in a panic as she ran down the stairs.

Judith fled from the storage room and ran to get Marion. As she searched the house for Marion, her heart began to slow down. She began to think clearer and more logically. She also began to remember that her great, times nine, grandmother was a dressmaker who used mannequins to display the dresses that she made. Images of herself and her mother playing with the mannequins filled her head. Judith laughed at herself for being frightened by over-sized dolls.

When Judith went back to the attic, she hurried towards the mannequins. She shone the flashlight on the dolls' faces and then laughed with relief as she squeezed the lifeless, cold arm.

Judith smiled to herself as she began to clean out the boxes that were filled with old clothing. She loved it when she got a good fright.

* * *

Judith went back to the attic the next day. Although she'd spent the whole of yesterday cleaning and sorting the items in the attic, there was still a lot more work to be done.

Judith wouldn't admit it to her parents, but she was actually having fun looking through the clothing that belonged to her ancestors. Of course, she didn't have the chance to talk to her parents since the incident two nights ago. Both of them seemed to be avoiding her. Judith sighed, realizing that it was more peaceful to stay away from her parents than to start a feud.

Trying to push the unhappy thoughts from her head, Judith made her way to the back of the attic. She carefully lifted an old dusty cloth from the top of an object. Judith's eyes went wide when she saw an old-fashioned trunk underneath the cloth. The trunk was made from a very dark wood and, upon closer investigation, she realized it had once been painted black.

Unable to suppress her curiosity any longer, she pried her fingers under the lid of the trunk. Judith groaned under the heavy weight, but the effort was well worth it when she saw what was inside. Tucked neatly away was a pile of black dresses. Judith gently unfolded a dress and studied it carefully. The dress was a faded color of black and had sharp cut fringes at the edge of the long-sleeved arms. Lace that re-sembled a spider's web ran along the low neck line. Judith ran her fingers over the cold fabric while wondering who had owned such a beautiful gothic dress.

Judith put the dress aside and began searching through the rest of the trunk. She looked in awe as she unfolded one beautiful black dress after another. When Judith picked up the last black dress and un-folded it, she heard a loud thud on the floor beside her. Then she began to cough furiously.

Judith felt her eyes itch and her throat burn. She waved one hand in front of her face while covering her mouth with the other hand. *Whatever fell from the dress disturbed the dust,* she thought, as she continued to cough.

The dust began to settle as Judith opened her eyes to see a black leather book lying at her feet. She let out a few more coughs as she bent down to pick it up. Just like everything else in the attic, the book was very cold to touch. Judith opened the book and then began to read.

This journal is the property of Ms. Judith Hyacinth Forge.

She stopped reading as her blood went ice cold. Judith never knew she was named after one of her ancestors. She swallowed hard as she thought about the likelihood of finding a journal that belonged to someone with the exact same name as herself. In curiosity, fear and excitement, she turned the next page.

June 28th, 1611. I received this journal as a birthday present from my dear older sister, Iris. I am so excited about turning nineteen today because it signifies the path to adulthood that I am about to take. The most exciting thing about being an adult is being able to be who I really am. I want to show the world the real me. Iris and I are very much alike, but she is afraid to admit who she really is. She is the sensible one and has spent endless hours lecturing me on why we must keep our true identity a secret. Iris believes that if we tell Mother and Father, as well as their friends, that we are witches they will disown and perhaps kill us. But I don't believe that. I know my mother and father will accept me as I am.

Judith stopped reading and tried to process what she'd just learned. She remembered seeing the name Iris Forge on the family tree diagram that hung in her father's study, but there were no records of a Judith Hyacinth Forge, other than herself, of course. Judith realized that Iris was her great, times nine, grandmother who was the dressmaker that used the mannequins. A shiver went down Judith's spine as she realized Iris never had a sister. Hoping the answers would be written in the journal, she began to read again.

As a birthday present to myself, I made a beautiful dress out of black fabric. Oh, the bother I endured to obtain fabric in the color of black. Such fabric is considered satanic. I strongly disagree. Although I practice magic and consider myself to be a witch, I certainly do not participate in any evil deeds. I use my magic for good and perhaps some light-hearted fun. I wish people could see that witches are not bad people. Let me correct myself – people will see that witches are not bad people. And I will be the one to prove it!

Judith closed the journal. Her head was racing with so many thoughts that she needed a minute to gather them all into logical sentences. She wondered what had happened to make Judith not be included in the family tree. She also wondered if the connection between her and her ancestor's name was just a coincidence. What she wondered the most, however, was how her ancestors had become witches in the first place. Judith had always been interested in fictional witches, but she never believed in them. Taking a deep breath, Judith opened the journal and began to read. She had a strong feeling that at least one of her questions would be answered in the journal.

June 29th, 1611. I am going to do it, journal! I am going to use my magic powers in front of my mother and father, and all their guests, at the dinner party my parents are hosting. I am not going to tell my sensible sister about my plan because I know that she would never allow me to do such a thing. I am going to wear the first black dress that I secretly made with my sister. I know I have other black dresses to choose from and that my first black dress is old and tattered, but that does not matter. That dress symbolizes my path to witchery. It was the first real thing that I was proud of. Tonight is the night that I, Judith Hyacinth Forge, will forever change prejudice against witches.

Judith stopped reading as she turned the page and saw that it was blank. She flipped through the rest of the pages and sighed when she realized they too were blank.

"I'll never know for sure why her family rejected her, but I can take a guess. I bet Judith went ahead with her plan and used her magic in front of her parents and guests. They must have been so shocked and horrified that they disowned her. It's almost like what happened to me the other night. Ancestor Judith and I both wanted to show everyone our true selves, but they shunned us. I guess Grandmother Judith's parents went a bit further than mine did," Judith seethed to herself.

Judith folded the black dresses and put them back in the trunk. She wrapped the journal in one of the dresses and placed it in the trunk also. She wanted to keep the journal safe. She was sure that no one else had seen it. Judith was sad, however, that she would never find out what had happened in the end.

* * *

It took three full days of work to clean the attic and box the items for charity. Judith kept the trunk that contained the journal and the dresses well hidden at the back of the attic. She planned to try a dress on one day.

With Marion's help, Judith was able to get the boxes to the Pattersons. Mr. Patterson had been delighted to see such a large donation. Judith's face went red when he commented on the big heart she must have to donate so many items. However, her face went even redder when he wished her luck with the community play in which she was starring.

After her trip to the Pattersons, Judith felt so tired and embarrassed that she collapsed on her bed. She'd been resting for half an hour when her telephone rang.

"Hello?" she answered.

"Hey Judith! How are you doing?"

Judith didn't need to ask who was calling. It was Samantha, her only friend. She was also the only other gothic person at school. But unlike Judith, Samantha was much more open about her beliefs.

"Hi Samantha! I haven't talked to you since the last day of school. I'm okay, I guess. How are you?"

"I'm okay, I guess," Samantha said, unintentionally repeating Judith.

Judith smiled. She knew they were very much alike.

"My mom took my book of spells away from me after I threatened to turn my brother into a toad," Samantha continued. "So, you can imagine how bored I am. Do you want to hang out or something?"

"Sure, I can be over in twenty minutes," Judith answered.

"Um, actually," Samantha stuttered, "I don't think that's such a good idea. My mom is pretty mad at me. She says she wants me out of the house for a few hours. Is it okay if I come over to your place? That way we can practice the spells in your magic book."

"I guess so," Judith replied uncertainly. She knew her parents didn't like Samantha very much. They believed Samantha had influenced Judith to become gothic.

"Great! I'll see you in twenty minutes, okay?"

After Judith had hung up the telephone, she waited outside for Samantha to arrive. Soon, Judith saw a girl, who was wearing a black lace top, a short black skirt and red fishnet tights, coming down the street.

"Hi Samantha!" Judith called.

Samantha waved to Judith and then stopped walking to let a car pull up the driveway.

Judith felt her heart sink as she saw her mother come out of the car with a disgusted look on her face.

"Hello, Mrs. Forge," Samantha greeted pleasantly.

"Samantha," Mrs. Forge said with a tight smile. "That's quite an outfit you're wearing."

"Thank you," Samantha replied, not really sure if Mrs. Forge's comment should be taken as a compliment or an insult.

"Would you mind answering one question for me?" Mrs. Forge suddenly asked.

"What is it?" Samantha asked in confusion.

"What do your parents think about your eccentric clothing?"

"Mother!" Judith yelled in shock.

"It's okay. I actually get asked that question a lot," Samantha said, trying to hide her embarrassment. "My parents don't really like my choice of clothing, but they have accepted it and me."

"Your parents must be *very* understanding. I know I could never accept a child who dressed in such a foolish manner."

Judith felt hot tears sting her eyes.

"I...I think I better go home," Samantha said awkwardly.

"Yes, I think that would be a good idea," Mrs. Forge replied.

Judith watched in shock as Samantha walked away quickly. "I can't believe how you just insulted Samantha!" she cried.

"I didn't insult her," Mrs. Forge said, while flinging her hands in the air as if to dismiss the thought. "In fact, I might have smartened her up."

"She doesn't need smartened up. She's the smartest girl in my math, science and history class!"

"Don't make such a fuss," Mrs. Forge scolded her daughter. "I did you a favor by getting rid of that weird girl. You need to make friends with proper young ladies. I can introduce you to..."

"I don't care about your ideal young lady. I'm just like Samantha. When you insulted her, you insulted me also. Why do you have to judge those who don't mimic your beliefs?" With that said, Judith raced into the house and up to the attic.

Judith didn't know why, but as soon as she'd entered the attic she ran to the trunk and pulled out the black dress. She hurried to place the dress over her head and pull it down over her body. Judith instantly felt better when she thought about her ancestor Judith. She knew her ancestor had gone through the same problems with her parents as she had.

Judith looked at the black dress she was wearing and smiled with pride. She felt an overwhelming connection with ancestor Judith. Judith stared at the black dress as she twirled around. She felt hypnotized by its blackness and smooth fabric. Suddenly, her surroundings started to spin. They spun so fast that everything became a blur.

"What's happening?" Judith cried, just before everything went black.

Judith's head throbbed as she opened her eyes. It took a few minutes, but her head stopped throbbing and she eventually regained her vision.

"What am I doing here?" Judith asked out loud, realizing that she was lying on the attic's floor.

As Judith got to her feet, she also realized that the attic looked different. The three mannequins were dressed in lavish flower print dresses. Tools, which a dressmaker would use, were sprawled on the floor as if someone had recently been working on them. Judith also noticed that there were old-fashioned trunks all around the attic. She shivered as she realized that the attic had definitely changed. Judith backed up towards the attic's exit and then began to run.

As Judith ran out of the storage room and throughout the other rooms, her heart raced. All the rooms were different. She knew she was in the right house; she just didn't know why it had changed.

"I have to see my room," Judith suddenly said aloud.

She was about to burst into her room, but stopped when she heard voices coming from inside. Judith quietly approached the room and peered through the crack of the slightly opened door. She almost screamed when she saw herself talking to someone.

"Judith, we have to keep this a secret," the person talking to the Judith look-a-like said.

"How can we possibly keep such an incredible discovery a secret, Iris?" the Judith look-a-like replied. "We have just invented a spell that works!"

"I realize that," Iris sighed. "But do *you* realize what that makes us?"

"We are powerful witches who can successfully cast any spell that we wish!" the Judith look-a-like cried enthusiastically.

"Shhh..." Iris warned. "No one can find out that we're witches. They would kill us if they knew."

Judith let out a small gasp. Somehow she'd traveled back in time to when her great, times nine, grandmother was a teenager. Beads of sweat began to form on Judith's hairline. She felt her throat tighten and she found it difficult to breath. Her whole body tingled in fear. All Judith could think about was getting home to the year 2011.

Judith had just turned her back on the bedroom when a hand grabbed her from behind. She was about to let out a scream when the same hand clasped over her mouth. Judith felt the person turn her around. Her eyes went wide as she came face-to-face with her grandmother Iris. With bulging eyes, Judith watched Iris signal for her to be quiet and follow her. Judith did as she was told and followed her into a room that was used as a guestroom in the year 2011.

"I've been waiting for you to arrive," Iris said, before shutting the door.

Judith gulped as Iris walked towards her with arms wide open. *She's going to strangle me,* she thought in horror. But to her surprise, Iris embraced her.

"My dear sister," Iris muttered in Judith's ear.

"I'm not your sister. I'm your very distant grand-daughter. I know I look like your sister, but I'm not."

"You *are* my sister," Iris replied. "You are my sister four hundred years from now."

"That can't be," Judith said in shock.

"There are a lot of things that I need to tell you," Iris began. "When my sister and I were walking in the woods one day, we found a man in dire need of help. His leg was caught in a fox trap. We helped him out of the trap and back to his house in the woods. We went there everyday and nursed him back to health. One day, he presented us with the gift of witchery. He taught us basic magic skills, but also how to think for ourselves and conjure spells. Soon, my sister and I had become independent witches with powerful magic. My sister, Judith, wanted to tell everyone about her powers, but I knew better. I begged her not to tell anyone, but she did it anyway. Her foolishness almost killed her."

"What happened?" Judith asked breathlessly.

"Before they could kill Judith, I cast my most powerful spell ever," Iris continued sadly. "I made Judith not my sister but born four hundred years later. That way my sister didn't exist now and she couldn't reveal our secret. However, the spell did not work perfectly. Magical guilt plagued me day and night. The guilt spell was cast upon me by the man in the woods because I broke a cardinal rule of witchery. Fortunately, the man had his spell cast back on himself. He suffered from magical guilt for casting a mean spell on someone who had saved his life. To call a truce and stop the haywire crossing of spells, the man agreed to cast one final spell that would allow you, the future Judith, to come back and stop the original Judith from telling anyone that she is a witch. That way I would have never cast the spell in the first place."

Judith stared at Iris with her mouth wide open. "Are you serious?" she asked bluntly.

"I am deadly serious," Iris replied with a stone cold expression.

"How can the original Judith be here now if I'm here also?"

"I haven't cast the spell yet," Iris explained.

"If you haven't cast the spell yet, how can I be alive?"

"I'm sorry, but I can't answer those questions. You would have to understand the reasoning behind spells and the consequences of them to understand the events that are happening."

"Okay, okay," Judith said, throwing her hands up in the air. "I don't think I'm ready to understand magic, so just tell me what I should do to save ancestor Judith."

"By the rules of magic you are the only one who can save my sister by convincing her to keep quiet."

"But how do I get her to keep her mouth shut?"

"I can't answer that. You have to figure out a way by yourself."

Judith had experienced so many weird things in the last hour that she no longer doubted anything.

"I'm starting to hate magic," she sighed.

Judith only had four hours to figure out a plan that would stop ancestor Judith from revealing herself as a witch. Iris had hidden Judith in her bedroom and told her not to come out until she was ready to put her plan into action.

Now, Judith took a deep breath as she peered out from behind Iris' bedroom door and then quietly walked down the hall to ancestor Judith's bedroom.

She took another deep breath as she tried to calm her racing heart. Then she ran into ancestor Judith's bedroom and yelled, "Hold it right there!" Judith blinked when she saw that no one was in the room. She had expected to see ancestor Judith.

Judith walked over to a desk when she saw the familiar black leather journal sitting there. She opened it and began to read.

June 29ᵗʰ 1611. I am going to do it, journal! I am going to use my magic powers in front of my mother and father, and all their guests, at the dinner party my parents are hosting.

Judith closed the book with a thud. She didn't need to read the rest – she remembered it all too well.

Where is she? Judith questioned in a panic as she tip-toed to the door. She thought she heard people talking. Carefully, Judith slipped out from the bedroom and crept towards the long staircase. Down below, she could see maids scurrying around in urgency. *They must be getting the dinner party ready,* Judith thought, realizing that she was running out of time. She hurried towards the attic, hoping that ancestor Judith was there.

Judith's heart began to race as she entered the storage room and saw that the stairs to the attic had been pulled down. Her hands clutched the thick brown rope she'd found in one of the closets. As she climbed the stairs to the attic, she realized they weren't rickety like they were in the year 2011. Judith climbed in confidence until she spotted ancestor Judith trying on a black dress.

As quietly as she could, Judith crept towards her. She tried to unravel the rope in her hands, but it fell to the floor with a thud. She froze in terror as she watched ancestor Judith turn around and stare at her with wide eyes.

"Oh my..." ancestor Judith began to say.

Quickly, Judith covered ancestor Judith's mouth with her hands. Judith hated herself for what she was about to do, but she knew she had no other choice. She roughly pushed ancestor Judith towards one of the big trunks that filled the attic. Ancestor Judith crashed against the trunk with a sickening thud. Judith winced but continued to work fast. She quickly pulled out a long, thin piece of black fabric which she had found in the house and then tied it around her mouth. Judith felt her heart ache as ancestor Judith moaned and weakly kicked her legs. Judith grabbed the rope that had fallen to the floor and tied it snugly around ancestor Judith and the trunk. When she was certain that ancestor Judith was tied securely, she ran from the attic and towards her bedroom. She knew she didn't have much time left.

"Judith, dear, you look absolutely wonderful," the mother of ancestor Judith commented.

"Thank you, Mother," Judith said politely, while wearing a fake smile. Out of the corner of her eye, she saw Iris smiling gratefully at her. However, Judith also thought she saw a hint of sadness.

After Judith had trapped ancestor Judith in the attic, she had run to her bedroom and changed into a pink and yellow dress.

The dinner party seemed to last for hours. Despite all the unusual events that had happened today, Judith was bored out of her mind. She could have kissed the wooden floor when the guests began to leave.

"You may go to your room and get ready for bed," ancestor Judith's mother told her.

Judith got up from the chesterfield and began to walk to her bedroom.

"Oh, Judith!" ancestor Judith's mother called.

Judith turned around, afraid of what she might hear. "Yes, Mother?" she asked with a lump in her throat.

"Thank you for behaving so well tonight. You were certainly on your best behavior."

"Oh, it was no problem," Judith smiled. "No problem whatsoever."

"Thank you for all your help," Iris said to Judith, after they had entered the attic.

"I'm glad I could help save ancestor Judith, but I'm sorry for having to constrain her like that," Judith said, casting her eyes in the direction of the tied-up Judith.

"You did what you had to do to keep her from coming to the dinner party – that's all that matters."

Judith smiled proudly, but the expression faded when she thought about how she would get home. "How do I get home?" she voiced her concerns.

"I'll fix that," Iris said sadly. "I only need to cast one more spell." Suddenly, Iris threw her arms wildly in the air and began to chant. "Oh, man of the woods, the spell is complete. Undo the spells that were once incomplete. Make my actions, and yours likewise, never have happened and forever be disguised. Let there only be one Judith Hyacinth Forge – the one who existed in the year of 1611."

Judith felt her stomach churn. She had a sickening feeling that she was about to get a bad deal from saving ancestor Judith.

"Make it be," Iris said quietly as she lowered her arms.

"No! Reverse the spell!" Judith screamed, right before she disappeared forever.

* * *

The Secret Oracle Of An Egyptian King

"Go...go away," fifteen-year-old Vaughan Riley stuttered.

The mummy ignored Vaughan and continued forward.

"It's all over for you," the mummy whispered in a dry voice. As he talked, the cloth covering his face moved up and down.

"What do you want from me?" Vaughan cried.

"You know what I want," the mummy snarled. "I want my treasure."

"I'll never give you the treasure!" Vaughan yelled bravely. "I've spent my whole life looking for it. Did you really think I would just hand it over?"

"Then I'll have to take it," the mummy threatened.

"No!" Vaughan screamed as he backed away from the advancing mummy.

"Stop this right now!" Dr. Riley shouted as he entered the room.

Vaughan and the mummy stopped to stare at Dr. Riley.

"Did we disturb you?" the mummy asked in a friendly voice as he pulled the white strips from around his head. "Sorry," he added in a sheepish voice, before Dr. Riley had a chance to respond.

"Aren't you two a little old to be playing dress-up?" Dr. Riley asked sourly.

Vaughan looked down at his explorer outfit, which consisted of a wide brim hat, a dark green shirt, brown shorts and a belt that held a small chisel. He then looked at his best friend, Danny, who was wrapped in toilet paper.

"We're not playing dress-up – we're actors," Vaughan protested, trying to hide his embarrassment over the realization that perhaps they were too old to be playing make-believe.

"I don't care what you call it," Dr. Riley snapped. "Just stop it right now." With that said, he marched out of the room.

The two boys said nothing as they picked up the toilet paper trail that had begun to unravel when the "mummy" was about to attack the great explorer, Vaughan Riley.

"Is your dad alright?" Danny asked, finally breaking the silence. "He hasn't been himself lately."

"I've noticed," Vaughan sighed. "I guess he's stressed about the grand opening of the King Rhinkuhtan exhibit tomorrow."

Excitement suddenly rushed over Vaughan. Smiling, he thought about the event which had led Danny and him to dress up in the first place. Vaughan's father, Dr. Riley, had discovered the tomb of King Rhinkuhtan – Egypt's last king.

Vaughan and his father had moved to Cairo ten years ago when Dr. Riley was offered a job working with a team of Egypt's finest archaeologists. When Vaughan found out he was moving to Egypt, he was overwhelmed with excitement. This excitement hadn't disappeared; Vaughan loved visiting pyramids and looking at the artifacts his father found.

"You're probably right," Danny said thoughtfully. "After all, this is one of the biggest discoveries your dad has ever made."

Vaughan nodded in agreement as he picked up the last trail of toilet paper. *After my dad sees how great the exhibit is, he'll relax and return to his old self again,* he reassured himself.

* * *

Vaughan shifted uncomfortably beneath the dark blue suit he had outgrown last year. Unfortunately, there had been no time to buy a new one for the big occasion. He scanned the audience until he found Danny, who was laughing and pointing at him. Vaughan resisted the urge to stick out his tongue.

Vaughan, Dr. Riley, the four archaeologists who helped excavate Rhinkuhtan's tomb and the museum curator were all standing in front of the new King Rhinkuhtan exhibit.

All the guests were amazed by the golden artifacts. However, it was the item under the dark purple velvet covering that was the main attraction. Underneath lay the mummified body of King Rhinkuhtan.

Although Vaughan had already seen the mummy, a rush of excitement surged through him. He looked up at his father, expecting to see a wide smile on his face, but what Vaughan saw shocked him. Dr. Riley looked nervous and very guilty.

"And now, without further ado, I present the mummified body of King Rhinkuhtan!" the curator announced.

Vaughan stepped aside as his father and the four archaeologists walked towards the velvet rug and pulled it off. The sudden bright flashes from the cameras blinded Vaughan.

After everyone took a picture of King Rhinkuhtan's mummified body, the question and answer period began. The curator guided the archaeologists to a high table at the front of the main hall, while Vaughan was forced to sit with the crowd.

"You looked pretty nervous up there," Danny stated as Vaughan sat down beside him.

"Thanks for noticing," Vaughan replied, rolling his eyes. "Actually," he said in a serious tone, "I was more concerned about my dad than myself."

"He kept looking nervously around the room. It's like he's waiting for something bad to happen. Have you found out what's bothering him yet?"

"Not yet," Vaughan answered. "Ever since finding that tomb he's been acting so strange. I just don't get it. Finding King Rhinkuhtan's tomb is the best thing that could happen in his career, so why isn't he happy?"

"I wish I could help, but I don't think I can. You and your dad need to have a serious talk."

"Thanks. I think I'll take your advice," Vaughan said.

"It's the least I can do," Danny said with a sly smile. "After all, if it weren't for your dad, I wouldn't be seeing the King Rhinkuhtan display until tomorrow."

The room became silent as the question and answer session finally began.

"My question is for Dr. Riley," a man who held a mini recorder said. "How did you discover King Rhinkuhtan's tomb?"

"We began the excavations after detecting a large empty space beneath the sand," Dr. Riley answered. "Finding the entrance to the tomb required sophisticated machinery and a lot of human will. When we found the entrance, finding King Rhinkuhtan wasn't too difficult."

"It was surprisingly easy," one of the woman archaeologists said. "We were prepared to deal with traps and false tombs, but found no such thing. I've been involved in many excavations and have never seen a tomb quite like this one."

"If the tomb was poorly designed, how can you be sure it really is King Rhinkuhtan's tomb?" the man who had spoken earlier asked.

"It *is* King Rhinkuhtan's tomb!" Dr. Riley suddenly screamed as he jumped up from his chair. "We've done carbon testing on the mummy and it is King Rhinkuhtan!"

Vaughan looked at Danny in shock, who returned his friend's stare. Murmurs of confusion echoed throughout the room while the other archaeologists tried to calm Dr. Riley down.

"I'm...I'm sorry," Dr. Riley stuttered. "I just want to make sure you realize the absurdity of your accusation. It's...it's not true. The tomb belongs to King Rhinkuhtan."

Suddenly, Dr. Riley hurried down from the stage and ran from the room.

Vaughan jumped from his seat and ran after his father. "Dad, wait up!" he shouted, following him all the way to their minivan.

"Get inside now!" Dr. Riley shouted to Vaughan, holding the door open for him.

Vaughan jumped into the van and closed the door. Dr. Riley inserted the key and then sped off.

Nothing was said until they rushed into their house.

"Mind telling me what just happened?" Vaughan asked breathlessly as he collapsed onto the kitchen chair.

"I...I can't," Dr. Riley answered as he locked the door and looked fearfully outside the window.

"When did you start stuttering?" Vaughan asked in annoyance. "There's obviously something going on. You might as well tell me now because I'll find out eventually."

"They're coming. I know they're coming."

"You're really starting to scare me," Vaughan said with a quivering chin. "Who's coming?"

Dr. Riley turned to face Vaughan for the first time since they had entered the house. "I don't know," he said sadly.

"Tell me," Vaughan pleaded.

"No, you don't understand. I really don't know who it is."

"Okay," Vaughan said slowly, trying to understand the situation. "You don't know who's after you, but do you know what that person wants?"

"They want the lie to be kept forever. They want everyone to keep believing that King Rhinkuhtan was the true king of Egypt."

"Of course King Rhinkuhtan was king!" Vaughan protested. "It's written in all the history books."

All of Egypt's citizens admired King Rhinkuhtan – he was known for being fair and helping even the lowliest of peasants. If what Dr. Riley said was true, many people would be devastated.

"He's not," Dr. Riley said, shaking his head. "In King Rhinkuhtan's tomb I found a scroll written in hieroglyphics. I was able to read most of it and discovered how the real King Rhinkuhtan was killed by his servant who then successfully impersonated him. No one knew except for the servant's brother, who was also a servant to the real King Rhinkuhtan. The servant's brother didn't like what was happening, but said nothing out of fear that he'd be killed. For the whole time that the fake King Rhinkuhtan ruled, his brother kept quiet. However, on the day that the fake king died, his brother recorded what really happened on the scroll and buried it alongside the fake king. He hoped that one day the truth would be revealed."

"Why didn't the brother verbally tell the truth after the imposter King Rhinkuhtan had died?" Vaughan asked in awe.

"He was afraid that people wouldn't believe him and then punish him for saying such things."

"Okay, so you found a scroll that changes Egypt's history, but you still haven't told me why someone would be after you."

"Someone was watching me on the day I discovered the scroll. He attacked just seconds after I had finished reading it. I fought back and eventually escaped. Although I still had the scroll, I didn't see my attacker since he was wearing a black mask. He must've been a part of the excavation since he had access to the tomb." Dr. Riley paused for a moment. "Then again, when I ran out of the tomb there were no security guards. Perhaps the man beat up the guards and gained entrance that way." Dr. Riley threw his hands up in confusion. "I don't know! The only thing I do know is that I brought the scroll home and put it in the safe."

"You did *what*?" Vaughan asked in shock.

"I didn't mean to steal the scroll," Dr. Riley protested. "I only wanted to protect it. When I took it to the carbon-testing lab, I was attacked again. This time a dagger was flung at me. Luckily, it missed. On the dagger was a note saying I was to burn the scroll and tell no one."

"So, that's why you've been acting so strange," Vaughan finally realized.

"I didn't want to tell you," Dr. Riley said, shaking his head sadly. "Now I'm afraid we're both in danger."

"What are we going to do?" Vaughan asked numbly.

"I can't tell the other archaeologists or even the police. I'll be thrown in jail if they find out."

"It's obvious that your attacker wants the scroll destroyed, so why not do it? Just burn it. It'll protect us, not to mention saving Cairo's citizens from the shocking fact that their beloved King Rhinkuhtan was a fraud and murderer."

"I can't destroy a ten thousand-year-old artifact!" Dr. Riley shrieked. "I took an oath that prevents me from bringing harm to an artifact."

"Then I don't know what to do. But you better do something. I have a feeling that the bad guy will be back."

As soon as Vaughan had finished his sentence, a loud bang on the front door startled them. They looked at each other in fear.

"Don't answer it," Vaughan pleaded.

Dr. Riley didn't have a chance to reply as a voice boomed from behind the door.

"It's Andy. Are you in there, Riley?"

Vaughan and his father let out a sigh of relief. Andy was one of Dr. Riley's teammates.

Dr. Riley opened the door and let Andy in.

"Is everything alright?" Andy asked in concern, after he'd been ushered into the house and then had the door closed behind him.

"Of course. Why do you ask?" Dr. Riley replied as he shot Andy a fake smile and then turned towards the window to look out fretfully.

"What happened at the museum?" Andy inquired. "Everyone's wondering."

"I...I felt sick," Dr. Riley lied. "I think I ate some expired clams or something. You better go in case it's contagious."

"Your excuse isn't making much sense," Andy said suddenly. "Are you sure there isn't something on your mind?"

Vaughan felt his chest tighten as he watched Andy closely. There was something about his cocky tone and expression that made Vaughan nervous.

"Talk to me, Riley," Andy said slyly, walking closer to Dr. Riley.

Vaughan felt his body tingle in fear.

"Could you please leave, Andy?" Dr. Riley asked in a funny voice, as if testing his friend. "I'm really not feeling well."

Andy shook his head slightly. "No, I don't think so," he hissed, coming closer to Dr. Riley.

Vaughan watched in horror as Andy reached into his jacket and revealed a dagger.

"Andy, no!" Dr. Riley said in disbelief.

"Oh yes," Andy replied as he leapt towards Dr. Riley.

Vaughan didn't have time to think as he ran towards Andy and kicked the dagger out of his hand. Andy looked stunned for a moment, but then he dived for the dagger. Fortunately, Vaughan was faster. He grabbed the dagger and held it in front of him.

"Put the dagger down," Andy said with less confidence.

"Not until you tell us what's going on," Vaughan challenged. "How could you attack my dad like that?"

"I wasn't going to hurt your father," Andy protested.

"Then why did you bring the dagger?" Dr. Riley asked angrily.

"To threaten you."

"Why?" Dr. Riley demanded.

"You know the truth about my ancestor," Andy snarled. "I had to stop you from ruining my reputation. Now, destroy that scroll."

"You want everyone to think you're so great because you're related to a king!" Vaughan yelled at Andy.

"No," Dr. Riley said abruptly. "I would've guessed right away that Andy was behind this if I had known that he was a descendant of King Rhinkuhtan. Why do you want to protect a name if people don't know about it?"

Andy's face suddenly went pale.

"Wait!" Vaughan shouted. "He's not King Rhinkuhtan's ancestor. My history book says that King Rhinkuhtan died without offspring!" Vaughan was still holding the dagger tightly. He liked the way it made him feel powerful.

"You're right!" Dr. Riley exclaimed, shaking his head as if he were angry with himself. "There's no way you can be King Rhinkuhtan's descendant. You were just a middle-class archaeologist until we found King Rhinkuhtan's tomb. What's really going on, Andy?"

Andy had just opened his mouth to answer when a loud crash from upstairs made Vaughan and Dr. Riley jump.

"What was that?" Dr. Riley asked with wide eyes.

"My back-up," Andy said with a confident smile.

Vaughan felt breathless as he ran towards the door and tried to unlock it with his free hand. Realizing that he needed both hands to escape, he dropped the dagger and opened the door. Vaughan felt awful about leaving his father, but he needed to get help from the police. There was no way they could fight Andy and his back-up alone.

Vaughan's legs and lungs ached, but he ignored the pain.

"You have to help me!" Vaughan yelled as he stumbled into the police headquarters.

Shocked, everyone in the building looked up at Vaughan and then rushed to his side.

"Get all your officers to 1786 Old Egypt Road now! I have an emergency. My father is being held up by at least two men."

The police officers didn't ask any questions until they were in the car, driving with the sirens on. "Why is your father being attacked? What state was he in when you left him? Do you know who is attacking your father?"

Vaughan answered the questions as thoroughly as he could, but his head was spinning from fear.

It seemed to take forever to get to Vaughan's house. He was told to stay in the car while the police officers investigated. Vaughan watched from the safety of the car, praying that his father would be alright and, if he was alright, that he wouldn't be in too much trouble for taking the artifact.

Horror swept over Vaughan when he saw Andy and an Egyptian man being dragged from the house in handcuffs. He looked on in admiration as the police officers restrained the two men. Vaughan's admiration was short-lived when he saw his father being escorted from their house in handcuffs.

"Why is my dad in handcuffs?" Vaughan yelled, unable to sit still any longer.

"He stole from King Rhinkuhtan's tomb," Andy said through a bleeding lip. "If I'm going down, he's coming with me!" he yelled, before being shoved into a police car that had just arrived.

Scared, Vaughan looked at his father. "No!" he protested. "You've got it all wrong. My dad was just protecting the scroll. He's not the bad guy!"

The police officers ignored Vaughan and proceeded to put Dr. Riley into the car.

"It's going to be okay," Dr. Riley reassured Vaughan.

"You better come with us," a police officer said to Vaughan.

Vaughan's heart raced. "I'm not being arrested, am I?"

"No, but we can't leave you here alone."

Vaughan felt numb as he was taken back to the police station. The recent events were too much for him to contemplate. Instead, he stared out the window and tried to think about nothing.

* * *

The police confiscated the scroll and Dr. Riley was forced to tell them everything. The story of Dr. Riley, Andy and, most importantly, the fake King Rhinkuhtan quickly leaked onto the streets of Cairo, where the citizens responded in an uproar. They needed someone to blame for the deterioration of the history they'd once been so proud of; Dr. Riley and the fellow archaeologists seemed like the most suitable people.

Dr. Riley was charged with harboring an ancient artifact and severely fined. He was no longer in trouble with the police, but his reputation was permanently scarred. Dr. Riley refused to leave the house and became even more withdrawn.

"I'm going to the grocery store!" Vaughan called to his father, taking the shopping list and money from the kitchen cabinet.

"Hurry back," Dr. Riley said, emerging from his study.

"I will," Vaughan promised as he walked out the door and shut it behind him.

Vaughan took a deep breath of hot, dry air. He was thankful to get out of the house. His father insisted that they spend most of their time inside and away from the angry citizens. Vaughan was beginning to wish that September would arrive; there was no way his father could keep him away from school.

Feeling the tense atmosphere, Vaughan quickened his pace as he walked through downtown Cairo.

"Pssst...Vaughan," someone whispered.

Vaughan spun around to see Danny sitting on a nearby bench, wearing sunglasses and a hat.

"Over here," Danny whispered again.

"It's not that hot," Vaughan said bitterly.

"Please don't be mad at me," Danny pleaded, once Vaughan had sat down beside him. "I wanted to see you, but my mom and dad wouldn't let me. They said I shouldn't talk to the people who ruined Egypt's history."

"I didn't ruin Egypt's history!" Vaughan exclaimed. "The real King Rhinkuhtan's servant did!"

"I know it's not your fault," Danny said with a sympathetic smile. "That's why I've been hanging out here all day – I was hoping to see you. I wanted to ask if you've heard about the excavation plans."

"What excavation plans?"

"I'll take that as a no," Danny said, biting his lower lip. "The Cairo museum has decided to hire a new team of archaeologists to excavate the real King Rhinkuhtan's tomb."

"Hold on a minute," Vaughan said, trying to get his head around the information he'd just obtained. "How do they know where the real tomb is? And why won't the museum hire the team that discovered the fake King Rhinkuhtan's tomb?"

Danny looked at Vaughan in sorrow. "The direction to the real King Rhinkuhtan's tomb was written on the scroll. As for why they hired another team," Danny paused and sighed, "I don't know how to say this, so I'll just spit it out – everyone knows your dad and his fellow archaeologists will never be given the chance to dig for artifacts again. No one believes that they can be trusted."

"That's crazy!" Vaughan yelled as he jumped up. "My dad made a mistake, but he isn't a thief."

"I know that," Danny replied. "It's just too bad that the rest of Egypt doesn't."

Vaughan glared at his friend, turned around quickly and then ran towards his house. He wasn't really angry with Danny since he was just telling the truth.

"What took you so long?" Dr. Riley asked as Vaughan came barging into the house. "And where are the groceries?"

"Forget the groceries," Vaughan said abruptly. "I just found out that the Cairo museum has hired a new team of archaeologists to excavate the real King Rhinkuhtan's tomb. The directions to the tomb were written on the scroll. Why didn't you tell me that,

Dad? And why didn't you tell me that you'd never work as an archaeologist in Cairo again?"

"I was so afraid this would happen. I knew the museum would want the real King Rhinkuhtan's tomb excavated, but I thought, perhaps, I would be assigned to the job. I've been a fool," Dr. Riley said, placing his head in his hands. "I'm sorry for not telling you about the scroll as soon as it happened. I wasn't thinking clearly."

"It's okay," Vaughan said, trying to sound reassuring. "But what will happen to us now?"

"We'll have to move. Perhaps I can get a job at the National Dinosaur Park."

"You're passionate about mummies and pyramids, not dinosaurs," Vaughan said sadly.

"I know, but we have to make the best of things," Dr. Riley said, ruffling Vaughan's hair. "Come on, let's get the groceries together. We can't hide forever."

Vaughan gave his father a weak smile and then followed him out of the house.

* * *

The months slowly went by and Vaughan regretted his wish for school to begin. No one seemed to like him anymore. Even the teachers, especially the history ones, gave him the cold shoulder. Vaughan's only friend was Danny. Grateful for Danny's company, Vaughan's respect for him heightened since he'd also become an outcast due to association. Vaughan was sure he'd miss Danny when he moved.

The Riley's house, which had been on the market for two months, had just received its first offer. Although thankful to be getting away from the cold stares, Vaughan would miss the beautiful deserts and pyramids.

The ill treatment of the Rileys had gotten worse during the past few weeks as the new archaeologists found and began excavating the real King Rhinkuhtan's tomb.

"Vaughan! Vaughan!" Danny shouted to his friend one morning in early October. "Did you hear the news?"

"What news?"

"The archaeologists entered King Rhinkuhtan's tomb late last night and then disappeared!"

"Disappeared?" Vaughan asked with wide eyes, suddenly grateful that his father was no longer working as an archaeologist in Cairo.

"Yeah, it's so weird. There were tons of video cameras recording the opening of the tomb. Then at exactly 11:23pm, the time when the seal to the tomb's entrance was broken, everything went black. All the safety lights burst into a thousand pieces! The archaeologists and the people recording the events had to make their way out of the tomb in the pitch dark. When they got outside, everyone was there except for the eight archaeologists! I can't believe you haven't heard! Everyone is talking about it."

"No one talks to me, remember?" Vaughan replied.

"Oh," Danny said awkwardly. "Anyway, they sent a bunch of people into the tomb to search for the archaeologists, but they came back empty-handed. The museum is calling for a new team of archaeologists to continue the excavation."

"This is ridiculous!" Vaughan exclaimed, throwing his hands in the air. "First my dad is targeted by two psychos, and then eight archaeologists disappear. Why won't the museum just give up on the excavation?"

"A lot of people believe that there is a curse on the tomb. They think the tomb your father found belonged to the real King Rhinkuhtan and that the king is angry at his people for doubting him."

"Enough!" Vaughan exclaimed. "I just don't care any more. My dad and I will be getting out of Egypt in a few weeks, and you know what? I'll be glad to go. I'll miss you, but not all this superstitious nonsense."

As Vaughan and Danny walked silently to school, Vaughan felt joy overpower him. *It's over,* he told himself. *I'm not going to worry any more.*

Vaughan quickly broke his promise of not worrying as he tossed and turned that night. He slipped into a restless sleep only to be awakened by a terrifying dream. Vaughan had nightmares that he and his father were being thrown out of Cairo by angry mobs. He'd almost fallen back to sleep when he heard a loud scream coming from down the hall.

"Dad!" Vaughan cried as he jumped out of bed and ran to his father's bedroom.

As soon as Vaughan entered his father's bedroom, he flicked on the light. When his eyes adjusted to the sudden brightness, he let out a bloodcurdling scream.

The Egyptian man, who'd been arrested with Andy, held a dagger to Dr. Riley's throat. Vaughan's sudden entrance stunned the man, but only for a few seconds.

75

"Don't move," the Egyptian commanded in a thick accent. "If you both do as I say, no one will get hurt."

Vaughan obediently followed the Egyptian man from the room and then out the house.

"I want you two walking in front of me," the man ordered.

"Where are we going?" Vaughan asked.

"We're going to the real King Rhinkuhtan's tomb," he hissed evilly.

One of us should make a run for it, Vaughan thought as he and his father walked side by side. *He wouldn't be able to catch us both if we ran in different directions.*

However, the image of the Egyptian man catching even one of them was too much for Vaughan to contemplate. Instead, he continued to walk.

It was dark outside and neither Vaughan nor Dr. Riley knew where the real King Rhinkuhtan's tomb was.

We're walking towards the original excavation site, Vaughan finally realized, noting that the newly dug tomb was also nearby.

Soon, they were at the excavation site which was well protected by security guards.

"How will we get inside?" Dr. Riley asked the Egyptian man.

The Egyptian said nothing as he turned to Vaughan and Dr. Riley and then smiled widely to reveal rotting teeth.

His teeth weren't like that before, were they? Vaughan questioned himself.

Vaughan and Dr. Riley watched in horror as an odorous, dark yellow gas seeped from the man's mouth. Horrifically, the weird gas surrounded Vaughan and Dr. Riley and left them frozen. All they could do was watch in fear as the Egyptian man walked towards the guards and blew in their faces. Soon, the guards were also frozen.

The Egyptian man returned to Vaughan and Dr. Riley. With eerie glowing eyes, he stared intensely at them.

Vaughan and Dr. Riley felt themselves melting and slowly regaining control over their movements.

Vaughan wanted to run for help; to tell the police about the escaped criminal and his weird features.

"Don't think about running away because you're going into the tomb," the Egyptian threatened Vaughan.

He can read my mind, Vaughan thought in horror. *How is this happening?*

"You'll have the answers once we get inside the tomb," the Egyptian said, reading Vaughan's mind once again.

Vaughan and Dr. Riley followed the Egyptian as he led them into the deep tomb.

The ground under their feet sloped down sharply, creating a strong feeling of vertigo. As the threesome walked deeper underground, the air began to get hotter and heavier.

The only light came from the glow of the Egyptian man's eyes.

Soon, they came to an opening in the wall. The remains of an old stone door lay on the ground.

"Go inside," the Egyptian commanded.

Not knowing what else to do, Vaughan and Dr. Riley followed the instructions. The Egyptian entered after them.

The room was old, dusty and empty. Vaughan and Dr. Riley watched in amazement as the Egyptian pried his fingers into a small crack in the wall and spread the walls apart. The whole room shook and sand began to sprinkle on them as the walls revealed a doorway.

"Follow me," the Egyptian instructed.

Vaughan was no longer scared. He had seen too much and no longer doubted the possibility of anything. Nevertheless, Vaughan felt his confidence dwindle as he saw eight people, who he presumed were the new archaeologist team, sitting in a corner of the room.

The archaeologists huddled together in fear when they saw the Egyptian man. However, they weren't the only ones in the room. In the corner – the area where the archaeologists were avoiding – was a mummified body.

"Please," Dr. Riley started to beg.

Dad's going to get us all out of this mess, Vaughan thought thankfully.

"Please," Dr. Riley continued, "I'll do whatever you want if you just tell me who you are."

Vaughan's mouth dropped open.

"I'll tell you who I am, but it will cost you your life!" the Egyptian answered passionately. "I am King Rhinkuhtan's servant."

"You...you can't be," Dr. Riley protested. "You died thousands of years ago. I just excavated your mummified body!"

"My mummified body may be in the Cairo museum, but my real body – my body that walks – is alive!"

"Tell us the story of what happened to the real King Rhinkuhtan," Dr. Riley pleaded desperately.

"Alright," the fake king replied. "I'd love to tell my brilliant plan to someone other than my ungrateful brother. I locked the real King Rhinkuhtan in this very room. Do you see that pathetic excuse for a mummy over there?" he asked, pointing to the mummy in the corner. "That's the real King Rhinku-htan. He doesn't look so great anymore, does he? I locked him in this room in early October. That's when a poisonous gas seeps through these walls. This phenomenon occurs every ten thousand years. And guess what? It's that time of year again." The fake king laughed, producing a horrible dry sound.

"How do you walk once again?" Dr. Riley pressed further.

The fake King Rhinkuhtan stopped laughing. "The cause of my rebirth is unknown. I remember the day I died and a long darkness. Then I arose on the day that my mummified body was found by you and your archaeologist friends. I took possession of Andy with my newfound powers and commanded him to get the scroll for me. Alas, he failed and I had to take action for myself."

"But you were arrested. How did you get out of jail?" Vaughan demanded.

The fake king laughed again. "I can move walls that weigh thousands of pounds. Getting past some thin metal bars and police officers wasn't much of a task."

"How did you fool your nation?" Dr. Riley asked with a bit too much enthusiasm.

"I was a fine impersonator," the fake king boasted. "I was a better king than the real one any-way – I was great to my nation. I took care of everyone, especially the poor. My brother never ap-preciated me. I woke up from my ten thousand year slumber to find that he'd written the truth about what happened. How could he betray me like that? We could've been so strong together if he'd only be-lieved in me."

"Why would he ever believe in a murderer?" Vaughan yelled as rage surged through his body.

"Enough!" the fake king shouted. "If Dr. Riley had just destroyed the scroll, no one would've found out the truth. Now that the truth is revealed, all I can do is take revenge on those who let the secret out." He backed out of the small room. "Goodbye," he said with an evil smirk as the wall began to close behind him.

"No!" Vaughan cried as he ran towards the wall seconds before it closed. He pried his fingers into the small cracks, but he didn't have the strength to open it. Vaughan turned to face the frightened archaeologists.

"I wish I hadn't taken this job," one of them muttered in fear.

"I wish I'd never moved here," Dr. Riley said in defeat.

"Don't give up," Vaughan encouraged. "If a ten thousand-year-old mummy can come back to life, we can surely find a way out of here. We just need to work together."

"We're too weak," one of the archaeologists complained. "We've been trapped in here for a day. We were almost out of air when the mummy opened the wall."

"You'll be even weaker when the poisonous gas comes," Vaughan stated.

No one moved. Even Dr. Riley looked hopeless.

"What's wrong with you people? Don't you want to live?" Vaughan asked as he turned back to the wall and attempted to pry it open once again. Beads of sweat formed on his forehead as he sunk his fingers deeper into the sandy wall and tugged with all his strength.

"What's that noise?" Vaughan asked suddenly as he heard a hissing sound. When he didn't receive a reply, he turned and looked at the others who were staring up at the ceiling in horror. As Vaughan looked up he felt his heart skip a beat. Seeping through the ceiling was a dark yellow, odorous gas.

"The poisonous gas!" one of the archaeologists screamed.

The horror was contagious as the seven other archaeologists began to scream as well.

Dr. Riley sat silently as if to die with dignity.

I'm not going to scream nor sit quietly, Vaughan resolved as he pulled his t-shirt over his nose and began to work on the wall again.

A minute had passed and the archaeologists were still screaming. Vaughan's ears rang from the sound of the archaeologists and the hissing of the gas. He was beginning to feel sick, but he still pried at the door.

Suddenly, the archaeologists' screams began to take on an even more frightened tone. Vaughan ignored them as he closed his eyes and pulled at the walls even harder. His eyes flew open as he felt the walls move apart. Then Vaughan finally began to join in on the screaming. Reaching from behind him was a pair of mummified arms.

Vaughan stumbled backwards and fell onto the mummified body of King Rhinkuhtan. The king made no sound as he moved away from Vaughan and spread the walls apart. The yellow gas that had begun to fill the air leaked from the room and dispersed.

When the archaeologists saw the open wall, they got over their weakness very quickly and jumped up from the floor. The archaeologist, who'd complained about being weaker than them all, was the first to leave the room. He was in such a hurry that he pushed the mummy over. The other archaeologists followed their friend, but in doing so they trampled over the fallen mummy.

"Are you alright?" Vaughan asked as he leaned on the ground next to the mummy. He couldn't believe he was asking a ten thousand-year-old mummy how he felt.

"Avenge my death," the mummy replied in a dry voice, before his head fell lifelessly to the ground.

"Let's get out of here," Dr. Riley said, coughing as he dragged his son from the room.

Vaughan and Dr. Riley raced out of the tomb and into the fresh air. The hot, dry air of Cairo had never felt so good to them.

"What's going on?" Vaughan asked for what felt like the hundredth time that day.

"It's unbelievable," Dr. Riley stated. "We'll talk about it later, but first we need to find that impostor before he hurts anyone else!"

"But he could be anywhere," Vaughan protested.

"I'm sure he's still in Egypt. No king, regardless of how he obtained the throne, would abandon his nation." Dr. Riley's face suddenly lit up. "I know where he is!"

"Where?" Vaughan begged for the answer.

"He's gone to collect his treasures."

Vaughan and Dr. Riley arrived at the Cairo museum half an hour later. Although Vaughan wanted to run, Dr. Riley made him walk. He said they needed to take deeps breaths to get rid of any gas that might have got into their lungs. He'd reassured Vaughan that they would be alright since they hadn't been exposed to the gas for a long period of time.

When they arrived at the museum's entrance, it was evident that it had been broken into. Even the security guards were frozen.

He's here, Vaughan gulped in fear.

"Wait here," Dr. Riley instructed Vaughan as he crept into the museum.

Dr. Riley moved closer to the fake king who was smashing the displays containing King Rhinkuhtan's gold items. He picked up a heavy gold bowl, which was sitting on a nearby pedestal, and walked slowly and quietly towards the fake king who was gathering small pieces from a broken display case. Dr. Riley raised the bowl and took aim. He threw it, completely missing his target as the fake king bent down to retrieve a piece of gold that he had dropped. The bowl smashed into a display case instead.

"How did you escape?" the fake king cried, grabbing Dr. Riley and pushing him towards the nearby display case that held the mummy's body. "You'll just have to take my place in here forever!"

Vaughan ran into the museum and towards his father and the fake king. He felt an unfamiliar strength surge through his body. Feeling like he had more power than ever before, Vaughan grabbed the fake king's waist and threw him against the display case.

Dr. Riley stumbled backwards and hit into a pedestal holding an ancient plate. The plate fell to the ground, crashing into a thousand pieces. The noise distracted the fake king for a moment. Vaughan took advantage of the fake king's shock and flipped him into the display case with his mummified body. Then he shut the lid.

Vaughan and Dr. Riley watched in amazement as the fake king struggled and shouted. Then he began to shrivel. Finally, the decaying mummy lay lifelessly in his case.

As Vaughan watched the fake king die, he felt his newfound strength being taken away from him. "I took your revenge," he whispered to the real King Rhinkuhtan.

"We better leave before the guards awaken," Dr. Riley said.

Vaughan nodded and then quickly followed his father.

"Let's just go to bed. We'll talk about everything in the morning," Dr. Riley said, once they were safely in their home. "We will need all the rest we can get. The news about tonight's events will be all over Cairo by tomorrow morning. I bet those archaeologists are already at the police station, telling them what happened."

"They probably won't believe them. Even I don't believe it," Vaughan added.

"You're in shock. So am I," Dr. Riley admitted. "Come on," he said, leading him up the stairs, "you need to get some sleep."

"There's just one thing I have to do first," Vaughan said with a wide smile.

"What is it?" Dr. Riley asked in surprise.

"I have to make a call," Vaughan replied as he walked towards the phone.

Dr. Riley nodded and then said goodnight.

"Hey, it's me," Vaughan said as Danny answered the phone. "Sorry for calling so late, but I have a really big story that I bet you haven't heard yet."

* * *

84

Cold Territory

Dale Stone smashed his ice axes and spiked boots into the icy mountain as he climbed higher. Resting for a moment, he looked down and estimated he was five hundred feet above the mountain's base. Dale smiled as the familiar feeling of pride and excitement surged through his body.

Climbing mountains was Dale's life. For years he had worked as a dentist, but after saving enough money, he quit his job and traveled to a faraway land in hopes of scaling one of the world's most deadly mountains.

With one hand, Dale took an ice screw from the pouch around his waist and drove it into the mountain. Then he clipped a rope around the ice screw. He did this to protect himself in case he fell but, of course, Dale the great mountain climber would never fall; the rope was just a mere precaution.

Dale took a deep breath as he continued climbing. He'd just driven his ice axes into the mountain and had started to dig his foot into the ice when he suddenly lost his footing. Dale's other foot slipped in the aftershock. He swung from the ice axes, trying desperately to hold on. Dale's arms ached and his fingers trembled, but even scarier was the way the ice axes moved under his weight.

"Hold on, Dale," he motivated himself, seconds before the ice axes slid out of the mountain and fell from his hands.

Dale crashed back and forth as he plummeted down the icy mountain. Suddenly, he was jerked upwards after falling past the second last ice screw he'd pinned into the mountainside. Using the rope to steady himself, Dale retrieved two emergency ice axes from his pouch and began to make his way back up to where he was before the fall.

Dale cursed to himself as he continued scaling the mountain. He couldn't believe he'd both fallen and lost his ice axes in a matter of seconds. Now in a bad mood, the climb felt even more difficult. His heavy clothing and weight from his backpack caused Dale to break out in a sweat. A cold wind beat upon the portion of his face that was exposed.

Finally, Dale neared the top of the mountain. With one last burst of strength, he flung himself onto the peak.

Pride swelled within Dale as he lay on the cold snow and stared at the blue sky. White clouds covered the tips of the higher mountains in the distance. His breath came out in small, white clouds and then drifted off. It was chilly on top of the mountain, but the bright sun warmed Dale. He readjusted his mountain climbing sunglasses.

"I'll conquer you next," Dale promised as he pointed his index finger towards the highest mountain.

Dale walked to the center of the mountain to take pictures of his surroundings. He was about to take a self-portrait when he heard a loud cracking from beneath his feet. Dale's eyes widened with horror as the snow cracked in jagged edges around his feet. He was about to jump, but he was too slow. As the snow gave way under his feet, visions of beautiful mountains and the blue sky disappeared from his sight. Dale was falling into the mountain.

A few seconds later, Dale landed with a thud on lightly packed snow. He shut his eyes tightly as pain and adrenaline coursed through his body. When the pain began to subside, Dale opened his eyes and then screamed in horror. Complete whiteness surrounded him. He turned his head from right to left, but still, everything was white.

"Oh," Dale moaned, as his head pulsated.

On his hands and knees, Dale searched for anything that might have fallen alongside him. It didn't take him long to find his backpack. Sighing with relief, he clung tightly onto it and continued searching. When Dale found his sunglasses, he quickly put them on and then gasped. Everything was a sparkling shade of white.

"It's the purest snow I've ever seen," Dale whispered.

Dale gazed at the snowy walls as he spun around. He was in a small room that had two exits. One of these exits was a dark hole in the wall, while the other was a small hole about fifty feet above his head.

I must have fallen through there, Dale realized. *I could've broken every bone in my body or even died!*

Dale looked at where he had fallen. The snow that broke his fall was lightly packed, so if someone fell they wouldn't be seriously hurt.

Does that mean I'm not alone down here? Dale wondered with a shiver.

Although his eyesight was still adjusting to the bright snow, he could see fairly well. Dale checked his equipment; he had fallen down with everything except his camera and ice axes.

I should explore this place, Dale reasoned. *And I better find another way out!*

Dale secured his belongings in his backpack and then headed to the hole in the icy wall. He gulped as he stepped into the darkness.

Dale could feel the brightness of the previous room leave him as he limped slightly in the dark. He took off his sunglasses, which made the room a bit lighter. However, it was still very dark as he bumped into a wall. Dale turned around and bumped into another wall. He touched the cold wall and began walking until he felt an opening in the hard snow wall. Not knowing where the path led, Dale stepped forward. He sighed as brightness filled his eyes once again. Dale was back where he had started.

Realizing that the only way out was through the hole in which he had fallen, Dale irrationally ran towards the wall and dug his spiked boots hard against the wall. Pain shot through his left foot, but he ignored the feeling and dug his other foot into the wall. Dale felt his muscles ache as he began to climb up the wall. He had only advanced by a few feet when he tumbled down. Dale landed hard on his back.

In a state of hopelessness, Dale took off his backpack to retrieve an energy bar. He ate it slowly, while thinking about the disastrous situation he was in. As Dale sat there, the cold temperature chilled his exposed face. It felt airless and silent inside the mountain. Dale only heard a quiet ringing in his ears, the deep breaths he took, and the beating of his heart.

It's actually kind of peaceful down here, Dale thought as he placed his backpack against the corner of the wall and leaned on it. He could feel his eyes getting heavy as his head tilted towards his chest. He closed his eyes and fell into a restless sleep.

Slowly, Dale began to wake up. Still half asleep, he muttered nonsense to himself and kicked his legs. He felt warm underneath a thick, soft blanket.

"Huh?" Dale cried aloud as he regained full consciousness. He remembered falling down the middle of the mountain and into a bright cave. He also remembered going to sleep with just his backpack for comfort; there had been no blanket.

Realizing that he wasn't alone, Dale jumped up and grabbed his backpack. He ran into the dark tunnel, determined to find a way out. However, as soon as Dale stepped into the darkness, he collided with someone.

"I thought I heard you," a deep voice said.

Dale's head spun as he stumbled out of the dark tunnel.

The man who'd just spoken advanced into the brightness. He stood tall at six feet and wore a robe made from the same material as the blanket. His face was a pale shade of blue and his white hair and beard were long and stringy.

"Who...who are you?" Dale stuttered in shock.

"I'm Yurick," the man replied, while smiling and offering his hand to Dale.

Dale didn't notice Yurick's hand. Instead, he stared at Yurick's teeth which were made from light blue jewels.

"Aren't you going to shake my hand?" Yurick asked with a booming laugh.

Dale finally shook Yurick's hand, but he never took his eyes off the strange man's teeth.

"Are we in the middle of the mountain?" Dale asked numbly.

"Yes," Yurick replied casually as he walked towards the blanket and folded it. "I was surprised to find you down here," he admitted. "I don't usually check this room, but I'm glad I did. You didn't hurt yourself when you fell through the hole, did you?"

"No, I...I'm fine," Dale replied, still stumbling over his words.

"Good," Yurick said with a smile, revealing his sparkling blue teeth once again. "Did my blanket keep you warm?"

"Yes," Dale answered, regaining some composure. "How long have you been down here? Do you still have your ice axes?"

"I lost my ice axes twenty one years ago," Yurick laughed. "It would be pointless to search for them now."

"Twenty one years! How have you survived for that long?"

"I was taught," Yurick said proudly.

"Are there more people down here?"

"Not anymore," Yurick said sadly. "It's just you and me. The real inhabitants of the Palace of Ice are dead."

Dale closed his eyes and prayed for his head to stop spinning.

"You don't look very well," Yurick observed. "Would you like some fresh ice water?"

"No," Dale said, slowly opening his eyes, "but I do want to know all about the Palace of Ice and its inhabitants."

"Are you sure? It's such a sad story."

"Tell me," Dale pleaded, suddenly realizing that he had made a discovery of a lifetime.

"Alright," Yurick agreed, unfolding the blanket and spreading it on the ground. He sat on it and motioned for Dale to do the same. Dale obediently followed Yurick's gesture and waited anxiously for him to start talking.

"As an avid climber, I was anxious to tackle this mountain. It was an unusually hot day when I started my climb, but I didn't want to turn back. It was hard work to get to the summit, but I finally did. I was standing on the peak of the mountain, looking at the beautiful scenery and feeling so proud. Then I heard the cracking of ice. The next thing I knew, I was inside the mountain and both my legs were broken. I remember lying on the ice cold floor in complete agony. I thought I was a goner."

"Go on," Dale urged when Yurick paused for a moment.

"Then they found me – a community of mountain inhabitants who called themselves Iceneeks. They looked human, only shorter, bluer, and with teeth made from jewels. The Iceneeks spoke English and reassured me that everything would be alright. Then they led me through a dark tunnel and into the most beautiful place I'd ever seen. They nursed me back to health and then taught me how to survive in the Palace of Ice."

"Why didn't you try to escape?" Dale asked.

"Once my leg healed, I tried to climb out several times, but it was useless. The Iceneeks didn't have the right equipment to get me out, so I finally gave up."

"You mean there's no way out of here?" Dale shuddered.

"Of course not," Yurick said angrily. "I've tried everything. Although this place is beautiful, I miss the real world. I'm so lonely."

"What happened to the Iceneeks?"

"I'm so ashamed," Yurick said in a tone that was barely audible. "I never meant to hurt them."

"I believe you," Dale said cautiously, realizing that he had no idea what kind of man he was dealing with.

"The change in temperature gave me a bad cold. Once again, the Iceneeks nursed me back to health, but in doing so they caught my cold. I guess they weren't immune to my germs because soon they were all dead." Yurick stopped talking to bury his head in his hands. "I feel guilty about it to this very day."

"Show me the rest of this place," Dale urged, not sure what else to say.

"Alright," Yurick agreed, perking up a bit.

Dale followed Yurick as he led him towards the dark tunnel's entrance.

"Stay close to me," Yurick warned. "It's very easy to get lost in these tunnels."

As Dale stepped into the darkness, he felt the air getting warmer. He moved slowly, putting one foot just inches before the other. The only sound came from Yurick's heavy breathing.

Yurick began to make quick, jagged movements. His speed increased until a bright light appeared at the end of the tunnel. Dale tried to peek around Yurick in the hopes of catching an early glance of the shimmering room. However, Yurick was too large, so Dale waited anxiously until he emerged from the tunnel after him.

"Oh, wow!" Dale exclaimed.

Pure white ice walls, decorated with flawless blue and red gems surrounded Dale. A pond in the far corner shone a brilliant shade of light blue. As if by a supernatural force, sunbeams were projected from the pond, making the gems twinkle.

The room was very large and contained appliances that every house had. There were chairs, tables and beds. The only difference was that the furniture was made out of ice and had a thick blanket covering them.

"This place is unreal!" Dale exclaimed.

Yurick laughed. "Although it may look unreal, I assure you it's not. This is how I survive."

"What do you eat?" Dale asked in a rushed, anxious voice.

"I catch my food through the pond," Yurick explained. "I eat fish and seals. I use my tourmaline spear to catch them."

"Your *what* spear?"

"The handle is made from a long icicle while a tourmaline gem is used as the spearhead," Yurick explained as he hurried towards the pond and spear. "If made properly, the spear can last fifteen years."

"Where did all the gems come from?" Dale inquired as he stared greedily at the glistening tourmaline.

"They grow here, of course!" Yurick exclaimed as if Dale had asked the silliest question possible. "We only have two types of gems, but they grow in abundance." Yurick pointed to a cluster of blue gems that were buried deep inside the icy wall. "These are the tourmalines."

Dale bent down to touch a cluster of tourmalines that were poking through the wall. They were cold and very jagged. He suddenly understood how they could rip the thick skin of a seal.

"And these," Yurick said, interrupting Dale's thoughts, "are star rubies."

Dale looked at the gem Yurick was pointing to. It was a deep shade of red and shaped like an oval. Most interesting was the white lines in the ruby, which appeared to make a cross.

"They're really beautiful and I bet very rare. Why didn't the Iceneeks sell them?"

Wide-eyed, Yurick turned to Dale. "Iceneeks only used gems for survival. They would never sell them, even if they could get out of the Palace of Ice."

"Why?" Dale asked simply.

"Why?" Yurick repeated in horror. "Because this place is cursed by the spirits of past Iceneeks — that's why!"

Dale looked at Yurick and then laughed. "Yeah, right. I think you've been down here far too long."

With intensity, Yurick looked at Dale and then raised his spear. Dale's eyes widened as Yurick ran towards him with the tourmaline pointed forward. Dale leapt to the ground, covered his head with his hands and waited to be pierced to death.

The sound of splashing water made Dale look up in surprise. He saw Yurick pierce at something through the pond that lay beside him. Proudly, Yurick pulled the spear out of the water to reveal a squirming fish on the tip.

"Hungry?" Yurick asked.

Dale licked the plate that had contained cooked fish. He usually had good table manners, but there was something about eating from a pure ruby plate that made him disregard niceties.

"Enjoyed that, didn't you, Dale?" Yurick asked with a laugh.

With his head still buried in the plate, Dale nodded.

"We should get some sleep," Yurick suggested, noting how the light from the pond had dimmed.

Although the room was darker, the gems still glittered brightly. Dale felt as if he were floating through a starry night sky.

"You can take that one," Yurick said, pointing to a small bed that was covered with several blankets.

Not knowing what else to do, Dale followed Yurick's instructions. Still fully clothed, he got under the blanket and shut his eyes. He heard Yurick nestle into a nearby bed.

"Dale?" Yurick asked suddenly.

"Yeah?" Dale replied, trying to sound sleepy.

"I know you must be sad, but I want you to know that there is nothing to worry about. I'll teach you how to survive in the Palace of Ice. I'll even make you an outfit like mine tomorrow."

Dale said nothing. He wondered if Yurick really thought those words would reassure him. He shook his head, as if trying to clear his mind.

It doesn't matter what Yurick thinks, Dale thought, *because before sunrise I'll be out of here.*

Dale was still wide-awake an hour later. He lay anxiously in his bed, listening to the rhythm of Yurick's breathing. Then, ever so quietly, Dale climbed out of bed and headed towards the tourmalines and star rubies. He kneeled down beside the cluster of gems and stared at them greedily.

Dale's hands shook as he reached out and touched a star ruby. The top of the gem was frozen into wall, but he had already thought of the solution to that problem. He removed the matches he had taken from his backpack earlier that evening. Dale struck the match and heated the ice around the gem.

He let the burnt match fall to the ground and then carefully rocked the star ruby back and forth until it came loose. Dale smiled as he held the heavy gem; he suddenly felt very powerful.

A loud snore from Yurick made Dale work faster. He quickly placed the star ruby into his backpack and then removed several more. Next, he moved on to the tourmalines. Once Dale had all the gems he could carry, he crept towards the tunnel, hoping he would be able to find his way out.

Dale had great difficulty maneuvering throughout the tunnels, but after fifteen minutes of bumping into walls, he found the room in which he had fallen. Dale looked up to see a faint light from the hole.

Dale walked to the wall. Then he took two tourmalines and drove them into the icy wall. Dale was happy when the sharp edge of the tourmalines pierced the wall. Still wearing spiked boots, he began climbing.

Dale was moving up the wall slower than he had hoped, but it was a very difficult climb. As he reached the top, he urged himself not to look down. Dale realized the dangers of being so high off the ground without the proper safety equipment.

Getting over the small opening in the mountain was the hardest part of the climb. Panic struck Dale as he swayed back and forth. Desperately, he searched for a place to sink his boots into. Dale was hanging sideways as he used a burst of energy to throw himself over the hole.

Once on the mountaintop, Dale scrambled away from the hole. He stuffed the two tourmalines into his backpack and then grabbed the emergency ice axes that had been left there earlier that day. Too afraid to get close to the hole, Dale left his camera and hurried to prepare for the climb down the mountain.

With only the moon to provide light, Dale finally made it to the bottom of the mountain.

"I'd rather be on this side," Dale muttered.

Dale began his long walk back to town, all the while smiling as he thought about the gems which were weighing heavily in his backpack.

* * *

Dale spent the remaining days inside his hotel room, while anxiously waiting for the day when he could return home. He had considered calling the airline and asking for an earlier flight. However, he didn't want to draw attention to himself and he thought that fleeing the country might do just that.

Instead, Dale protectively watched his gems. He had individually wrapped each star ruby and tourmaline and carefully packed them into his suitcase. He hated the thought of having them out of his sight and exposed to the possible danger of theft, but he knew his best chance of smuggling the gems was through this method. Dale knew that the gems couldn't be taken on the airplane as hand luggage.

Dale's anxiety increased as the day of his flight approached. On the night of his last day there, Dale couldn't sleep. He stared at the ceiling and counted the tiles. When that didn't make him sleepy, he stared at the old peeling wallpaper and counted the small red flowers that decorated it. The red flowers became fuzzy and Dale's eyelids finally closed.

Suddenly, something cold and heavy swept over Dale.

Dale's heart raced as he woke up and looked around the room; everything appeared normal. He quickly glanced at his luggage and was relieved to see that it was still there. He lay back down in bed.

It was just a shadow from outside — probably a cat or something, Dale reasoned as he turned on his side and pressed his face into the warm pillow. *I can't wait until my gems and I are safely home.*

"Give them back," a hoarse voice said suddenly.

Dale sprang back up in bed, his eyes wide with fear.

"Take them back to where they belong," the voice said again.

Dale swung around in bed and surveyed the room. He saw nothing.

"Give them back to me," whispered the voice.

"Who are you?" Dale demanded.

A knock sounded and quickly became louder.

"Be quiet!" said an angry voice from behind the wall.

"Did you hear a voice?" Dale called, realizing that the knocking was coming from a disturbed neighbor. He repeated the question when he didn't receive an answer.

"Are you talking to me?" the voice behind the wall asked.

"Yes," Dale replied. "Did you hear that voice just a minute ago?"

"I didn't hear anything but your yelling," the neighbor responded. "Is everything okay?"

"I...I'm fine," Dale reassured him. "Sorry to disturb you. I must've had a bad dream."

"Keep it down," the neighbor said.

Dale lay back in bed yet again. He tried to convince himself that he really did have a nightmare and that there was no voice in his room. However, he wasn't convinced. He spent the night worrying and falling into short, restless sleep patterns.

* * *

Dale hadn't heard any more noises last night, but he was extremely tired as he dragged himself out of bed the next morning. Although he wanted to go home, he was nervous about going through the airport's security. He'd heard from many people that the airport had very strict rules. Dale shuddered as he thought about what would happen if the security guards caught him.

"Don't be so negative," Dale told himself. "You're not going to get caught."

"Next in line!" a security guard called as he motioned for Dale to step forward.

Dale removed his watch and flung it onto a nearby dish before stepping through the metal detector.

"Enjoy your flight," a woman said, handing Dale his watch after he'd successfully gone through the detector.

"Flight 521 is now boarding!" an automated voice boomed throughout the airport.

Nervously, Dale held the ticket in his sweaty hand and proceeded to the boarding area. He'd just got in line when a pair of hands slammed down on his shoulders.

"Hey!" Dale exclaimed, startled by the sudden attack.

"Hand over your bag," the police officer, who had grabbed Dale, demanded.

Dale didn't have a chance to succumb to the man's demand as the bag was roughly torn from his hands. His heart raced. He was thankful he hadn't put the gems in his hand luggage.

Dale watched as the officer unzipped his bag and rummaged through it. The officer's eyes widened and then he called into his walkie-talkie for back-up. Dale didn't have a chance to voice his confusion as another officer approached the scene and dragged Dale from the line.

"What's going on?" Dale finally choked out as he was pushed into a dark room.

The officer reached into Dale's bag once again. This time he revealed a star ruby.

"We received an anonymous tip," he said in a thick accent. "We were told that you had stolen many gems from our country."

"I didn't put that star ruby in my bag," Dale said truthfully.

The officer gave Dale a dirty look. "The rest of your luggage is being sent here."

"This isn't fair. You have to let me go." Dale felt panic rush over him. Although he was surprised to see the star ruby in his hand luggage, he knew exactly what would be found in his suitcase.

"Isn't fair?" the officer mocked nastily. "I'll tell you what isn't fair! How would you like some outsider to visit your country and steal gems from your museum?"

"Museum?" Dale muttered. "I never took any gems from a museum. I found them."

The officer looked at Dale with disgust. "How dare you insult my intelligence! Do you take me for a fool? Star rubies can't be found anywhere but in the museum. The last cluster was excavated over two hundred years ago."

"I've found lots of them, as well as tourmalines," Dale pleaded.

"So you admit it!" the officer exclaimed. "Last night the museum was robbed of all its star rubies and tourmalines."

The officer stopped talking as two more men, who were carrying Dale's luggage, entered the room. Dale watched in terror as the officer opened his luggage, unwrapped numerous packages, and revealed the star rubies and tourmalines. One of the officers nodded to another. Suddenly, the officers approached Dale and lifted him up. Then they proceeded to drag him out of the room.

"Where...where are you taking me?" Dale stuttered with shock.

"Where thieves like you belong," replied an officer as he shoved Dale outside and then into a car.

"You can't do this to me!" Dale shrieked. "I have rights! I deserve a trial!"

"A trial?" one of the officers mocked. "There is no trial for thieves like you. You get thrown straight into prison."

"No! I demand a lawyer!"

In a fury, Dale kicked one of the men. The man stumbled backwards and yelped with pain. Dale was about to jump out of the car when the other officer slammed the door shut. The door hit Dale's head and then everything went black.

When Dale woke up, his head was pounding. He was surrounded with darkness. When his eyes adjusted to the change in light, he realized that he was in a small room built from large gray stones. In the corner was a thin mattress lying on the floor; a thin, torn blanket lay in a heap on top of it. In the other corner was a toilet. Although the room was dark and gloomy, the thick metal bars that locked Dale in scared him the most.

"Let me out of here!" Dale yelled as he leapt towards the bars and shook them forcefully. He grabbed at the cluster of chains, which kept the bars closed, and tugged at them with all his might. The chains made a loud clunking noise against the bars, but they didn't come loose. "Let me out of here!" he yelled again.

"Why should I?" came a cold voice from behind Dale.

Dale shivered furiously. He was positive that there was no one else in the jail cell a minute ago. When Dale turned around, horror filled his eyes. He stared at a man whose face was hidden by a dark hood. All Dale could see was an outline of a pale blue face and the blinding brightness coming from his teeth. He was even clothed in the same outfit Yurick wore.

"Are you an Iceneek?" Dale asked, not really wanting to know the answer.

"Of course," the Iceneek snapped. "I'm the ghost who was chosen to protect the Palace of Ice from thieves. It's my duty to make sure our gems stay where they belong."

"You put that star ruby in my hand luggage," Dale realized, hardly believing what he was saying.

"Yes," the Iceneek confessed. "And I did a lot more than that. I broke into the museum and hid their star rubies and tourmalines. Then I called the police and told them that you were responsible for it and where you could be found."

"Listen, I'm really sorry that I stole your gems. I'll put all of them back – I promise." Dale felt beads of sweat dripping down his face. He couldn't believe that a ghost had set him up.

"It's too late to make amends," the Iceneek sneered. "Besides, I've already taken the gems back to the Palace of Ice. I have no further use for you. The police, however, will definitely need you. Now that the star rubies and tourmalines have been stolen yet again, they will think you have an ally. They'll be asking you a lot of questions which you won't be able to answer. I suppose you're smart enough to figure out what the consequences of that will be."

"No," Dale choked. "Please don't let them hurt me."

"The police are very proud of their heritage. They hate it when foreigners steal from them," the Iceneek hinted with a sinister tone.

"Please...I'm sorry," Dale pleaded. "Just don't let them hurt me."

"Stop repeating yourself – it's annoying," the Iceneek scolded. "I see that you're truly sorry, so I'll offer you a choice. You can stay here and be at the mercy of the police, or you can come back with me to the Palace of Ice."

"Will I have to live in the Palace of Ice forever?" Dale asked with wide eyes.

The Iceneek nodded.

"After what I've done to you, why would you want me to live in your beautiful palace?" Dale asked suspiciously.

"I don't make the rules," the Iceneek replied. "I truly wish you had never fallen inside the mountain, but it's too late to change that."

"Alright," Dale agreed. "I'll go back with you."

Dale watched in amazement as the Iceneek stepped closer to him and revealed the biggest and most beautiful tourmaline he had ever seen. Dale let out a startled cry as the tourmaline burst into a hundred pieces and released a blinding light. The next thing Dale knew was that he was back in the Palace of Ice, lying on the same snow mound that he had first fallen on.

"Hello, Dale," Yurick said in an unfriendly voice.

"Where's the Iceneek?" Dale demanded.

"He's gone. Iceneeks only come to fulfill their duties when something goes wrong."

"Oh," Dale said simply.

"You shouldn't have stolen those gems," Yurick scolded.

"I know," Dale said sincerely. "I wish I had never taken them. Please understand, Yurick, that I am truly sorry."

"Then make it up to me. Tell me how to get out of here."

Dale looked at Yurick with surprise. "You can't leave!"

"Yes I can, but only if you tell me how. I'm not going to steal any gems," Yurick added, when he saw Dale give him a suspicious gaze.

"You can't leave me down here. I don't know how to survive."

"I'll teach you everything you need to know," Yurick promised.

"I don't want to live here by myself."

"You should have thought about that before you stole the gems. Surely you knew that you would be punished."

"Fine, I'll help you," Dale agreed, not knowing what else to do.

* * *

Yurick spent the next four weeks teaching Dale everything he would need to know to survive. On the day of Yurick's departure, Dale was surprisingly relieved. Yurick had become bad-tempered and just plain annoying.

I guess being so close to freedom can really change a guy, Dale thought as he watched Yurick disappear through the mountain's opening.

Dale had just turned around and prepared to walk through the tunnels when he heard an unhappy voice mutter, "Dale, you've done it again." Emerging from the dark tunnel, surrounded in a bright blue light, was the Iceneek Dale had met before.

"What...what have I done?" Dale asked, while remembering Yurick telling him that Iceneeks only return when they have a duty to fulfill.

"You have let Yurick escape," the Iceneek replied angrily.

"So?" Dale asked with confusion. "I thought I was the only one who wasn't allowed to leave."

"You fool!" the Iceneek bellowed. "We wanted to keep Yurick here because he knows all our secrets. We told him that there was no way out so he would stay here forever. Now, he has gone back to the outside world and there is nothing that I can do about it."

"Why not?" Dale questioned. "You found me quick enough."

"Yes, but you did something wrong. Yurick is innocent."

"I'm sorry," Dale said pathetically.

"Well, I can't punish Yurick but..." the Iceneek stopped and stared at Dale, "I can punish you. I think it would be for the best if you came with us. You cause too much trouble when you're down here."

Dale shut his eyes as he felt a cold wave surge through his body.

When he opened his eyes, everything was bright. As his eyes adjusted to the brightness, he realized that he was high in the sky, looking down at the mountains. The Iceneek rested on the cloud in which Dale was sitting.

"We spend our days guarding the mountains," the Iceneek explained.

"I have to look at mountains forever?" Dale muttered.

The Iceneek gave him a sad nod.

"That's too bad," Dale said, trying to suppress a smile. "I really hate looking at mountains!"

* * *

Kingdom Of Sugar

Clayton Baxter didn't make a sound as he pressed his ear against the door and listened. He heard nothing but silence. Ever so carefully, Clayton placed a key into the lock and then gently pushed the door open.

Clayton's tense body relaxed when he saw that the room was dark and empty. Smiling to himself for getting away with such a devious plan, Clayton quietly jogged to his bedroom. He opened his bedroom door and then muffled a scream as someone clasped their hands over his mouth.

"How could you?" she asked as she released her grasp on Clayton and turned on the light switch.

Clayton spun around to see his mother. He tried to hide the brown paper bag behind his back, but he wasn't fast enough. Mrs. Baxter grabbed the bag and ripped it open.

"Oh," she moaned in disappointment, upon seeing the contents of the bag lying on the floor.

Ashamed, Clayton turned his head away from the mess. "I'm so sorry," he muttered.

Mrs. Baxter bent down and picked up the fallen candy wrappers.

Clayton couldn't watch his mother throw the handful of wrappers into the garbage can; he was too disgusted with himself.

"We need to have a serious talk," Mrs. Baxter said, motioning for her son to sit down in a nearby chair. "You promised me you would stop eating candy. However, it seems like you've been eating more than ever."

Clayton lowered his head in shame. "Yes, I have," he admitted. "I bought the candy just an hour ago and have already eaten it all. I'm a monster!"

Mrs. Baxter patted her sobbing son's back. "You aren't a monster," she reassured him. "You just have an extra sweet tooth."

"But I *am* a monster! I've broken my promise to you!"

"We can talk about this in the morning," Mrs. Baxter said, looking at the clock that read 10:10pm. "We'll create a sugar reduced diet and I'll make sure you stick to it." She smiled sympathetically. "Remember to brush your teeth before going to bed," she added before leaving his room.

Clayton changed into his pajamas, brushed his teeth, turned off the light and then climbed into bed. He tossed and turned, trying to get comfortable. However, no matter how hard he tried, he just couldn't relax. Clayton felt blood rush through his veins and his face flush. He turned on his side and moaned. Praying for his stomach to stop churning, Clayton fell into a restless sleep.

The sound of loud thudding awoke Clayton. At first he thought he was only dreaming, but when something hit him on the head and it hurt, Clayton knew he was awake.

Clayton screamed – he was no longer in his bedroom. Still in his pajamas, he jumped up to get a better look at his surroundings. However, in doing so, he tripped and fell on the object that had hit his head.

Clayton lay on the ground, next to a large gumdrop. Shakily, he sat up and examined the sugary treat.

The gumdrop, which was a light shade of green, was shaped like a teardrop. Covered in white sugar, it sparkled brilliantly whenever light hit it.

Although confused, Clayton was happy to find such a large candy. He was about to reach out and grab it when suddenly a red gumdrop hit him on the head.

"Ouch," Clayton moaned, while rubbing his head.

Then a yellow gumdrop hit him. Clayton let out a scream of terror as he looked up to see hundreds of gumdrops falling from the sky.

Clayton curled in a small ball and put his hands over his head. He cringed every time the large gumdrops hit his back. As the gumdrops continued to rain on Clayton, he realized he needed to find shelter.

He stood up and, keeping his head low, began to run.

Suddenly, Clayton spotted a house that looked like it was made from gingerbread. When he reached the house, he pounded on the door. Clayton waited for a few moments, but no one answered.

How did I get here? And where is here? Clayton questioned as he leaned against the side of the house.

The thick frosting that hung over the edge of the roof provided Clayton with some protection. He waited until the raining of gumdrops became less and then eventually stopped. Clayton looked in awe as the gumdrops melted into beautiful puddles of yellow, green, purple, red and blue.

Clayton stepped away from the gingerbread house to gaze upon it. The house stood only six feet tall and was fifty feet wide. The dark brown walls were held together by a thick white frosting; the same frosting that decorated the edge of the roof and hung down like icicles. The frosting also outlined the door and windows.

When Clayton heard a dripping noise, he turned his attention to the long candy cane drainpipe. Running down the drainpipe was the melted gumdrops. Clayton watched in fascination as the gumdrop goo gathered in a multi-colored puddle at the edge of the house. He kneeled down beside the puddle and stared at it.

"It's beautiful," Clayton said. He reached for the puddle of sugary goodness, all the while imagining how it would taste.

"Hold it right there!" a small voice screamed.

Terror-stricken, Clayton turned around slowly and then gasped in horror.

Standing in the doorway of the gingerbread house was a small gingerbread boy. Adorned with sparkly blue sugar, the gingerbread boy had silver balls for eyes and a mouth made from licorice. He stood small at three feet and had dark gingerbread skin. The most magnificent aspect of the gingerbread boy was his human characteristics. He was shaped like a boy and could move easily.

The gingerbread boy returned Clayton's stare. As he blinked, his silver ball eyes were momentarily covered by a thin layer of gingerbread.

"What are you? Where am I?" Clayton asked suddenly, no longer feeling tempted to eat anything that came from this strange place.

"You're in the Kingdom of Sugar. Don't you know anything?" the gingerbread boy asked, while rolling his silver ball eyes.

"How did I get here?" Clayton asked, feeling a lump grow in his throat.

"I can't tell you how you got here, but I can tell you why!" the gingerbread boy said with a bit too much enthusiasm as he moved closer to Clayton.

Feeling threatened, Clayton stepped backwards. "Alright, tell me why I'm here," he demanded, trying to sound brave.

"You've been chosen to come here because of your dedication to all things sugar," the gingerbread boy said smirking. "We want to repay you for your loyalty."

Clayton continued to move back as the gingerbread boy advanced towards him at a faster pace.

"Sugar tastes great, doesn't it? But I know something that tastes even better!"

"What?" Clayton asked, gulping in fear. He had a feeling that he wouldn't like the answer.

"Humans!" the gingerbread boy yelled, before leaping for Clayton.

Clayton quickly jumped out of the gingerbread boy's way. He watched in amazement as the gingerbread boy fell on the ground and into a gumdrop puddle. Clayton stared in horror as the gingerbread boy tried to pull himself from the puddle.

The puddle must be drying and turning sticky once again, Clayton thought.

"Help me!" the gingerbread boy pleaded.

"No chance!" Clayton yelled as he turned around and started running.

"I wasn't really going to eat you! I was just kidding!" the gingerbread boy called.

Just kidding? I don't think so. Clayton gulped hard as he ran through the strange land. He knew he was in real danger. Somehow, he'd entered a land full of sugary treats that liked to eat humans. "This is no joke," Clayton said over the sound of his thumping heart.

Clayton ran until he could run no more. Out of breath, he collapsed on the ground. For the first time since arriving in the Kingdom of Sugar, Clayton took a long look at his surroundings.

The blue sky and white clouds looked as if they were made from cotton candy, while the sun looked like a large orange lollipop. The bark on the trees looked like cracked gingerbread, and the leaves like green cotton candy. Even the ground was made from gingerbread and green cotton candy. Clayton had never seen so much candy before, but for some reason he wasn't tempted by it.

After resting for a little while, Clayton rose to his feet and began walking. Not wanting to go back and face the gingerbread boy, he headed down the long gingerbread path. The edge of the path was adorned with silver balls like the gingerbread boy's eyes. Clayton shuddered and tried not to look down. He imagined that the silver balls belonged to gingerbread people, who were watching him right now and going to attack at any moment. The scary thoughts made Clayton walk faster.

As Clayton held his head high, unwilling to look at the creepy silver balls, he saw a dark purple mountain rise high in the sky. White creamy foam sat on the tip of the mountain.

When Clayton reached the mountain's base, a brown sign made from gingerbread caught his attention. He read the candy cane writing out loud, "Jelly Mountain. Proceed at your own risk."

In fear, Clayton backed away from the mountain. He didn't like the way Jelly Mountain quivered and he certainly didn't like the way the foam was slowly sliding downwards.

Clayton shivered before turning to his left and walking along the base of the shaking purple mountain. He was upset to see that once he turned the corner, another Jelly Mountain was there. Clayton sighed in frustration when he realized that there were miles of mountains that rose high into the sky.

Deciding that he'd have more luck if he went back down the gingerbread path, Clayton turned around. He didn't know what he was looking for; he just knew he had to keep moving if he wanted to get out of the Kingdom of Sugar alive.

Clayton hadn't gone far when he heard a familiar shout. He gasped in horror upon seeing a gingerbread man and woman, along with the gingerbread boy who was covered in dried gumdrop liquid, running towards him. The very sight of the three angry gingerbread people would've made Clayton laugh if he weren't so scared.

Not knowing what else to do, Clayton ran back to Jelly Mountain. He gulped when he re-read the caution sign. Trying to ignore the intense fear that was coursing through his body, he jumped onto the mountain.

His hands and feet sank into Jelly Mountain first, followed by the rest of his body. Clayton took a deep breath as he prepared to be engulfed by the jelly. He closed his eyes and waited to die.

Clayton's eyes flew open when he felt his body hit against something hard. He stared down at his hands to see that he'd only fallen into Jelly Mountain by a couple of feet before the hard inner layer of the mountain stopped him. He sighed with relief, happy that he was safe.

Unfortunately, the feeling of security didn't last long when he heard the angry shouts of the gingerbread people. Clayton looked behind to see the gingerbread people only a few feet away from Jelly Mountain.

Seeing no alternative, Clayton began to climb the mountain. It was hard work dragging his body from the jelly; however, with a burst of strength, he managed to pull himself out of the sticky mess. Making sure that only his hands and feet touched the jelly, Clayton slowly made his way up the mountain. He looked behind once more and was pleased to see that the gingerbread people weren't following him.

"You'll never make it over these mountains!" the gingerbread boy shouted angrily. "And if by chance you do, you'll never survive the evil candy bears."

"You would've had a better chance if you faced us!" the gingerbread man snickered. "The candy bears have a bigger appetite than us!"

Clayton knew that the gingerbread people were shouting more terrifying warnings at him, but thankfully, he couldn't hear the rest of their words over the loud winds that blew high on the mountaintop.

Clayton scrambled to the top of Jelly Mountain.

Why would they think I couldn't climb this mountain? Clayton wondered as he reached the white foam.

Clayton suddenly realized why the gingerbread people had warned him about climbing the mountain. His hands, feet, and then whole body began to sink into the white foamy mountaintop. However, there was no longer a hard core to stop him from falling deep inside.

A surprisingly large amount of pressure from the white foam covered Clayton's body. He hadn't had the chance to take a deep breath before the foam engulfed him. Clayton's chest tightened and his lungs ached. Without thinking, he gulped for air. Instead of air, he got a mouthful of vanilla ice cream. Clayton was surprised to taste the sweetness as he swallowed it and then began swimming in the ice cream. He flung his arms back and forth, hoping to move towards the top of the mountain. He began to advance, but not by much.

Clayton's muscles were getting really sore and his chest felt like it was going to explode. He was sure that he was going to die. Clayton didn't know how far he had sunk into the mountain, but he knew he would never see the bright orange lollipop sun again.

This is the last chance I have to survive, Clayton told himself as he took a final surge of energy and propelled himself forward. He kicked and punched at the ice cream until he burst through the surface.

Clayton took a huge, and very much appreciated, breath of fresh air. Panic struck him as he began to sink back into the mountain. Not allowing himself to become stuck again, Clayton kicked his legs and flapped his arms until he was tumbling down the other side of the mountain.

Clayton formed himself into a ball so he wouldn't sink too far into the ice cream topped mountain. When he reached the purple part of Jelly Mountain, Clayton tried to loosen his body; however, he was going so fast that his body tightened into a smaller ball. He continued rolling down the mountain, while feeling the jelly gathering all over him.

Finally, Clayton reached the bottom of the mountain with a loud thud. He sat there in shock, throbbing all over.

Then Clayton started laughing hysterically. He didn't know why he was laughing. Perhaps, he laughed because he had come face-to-face with death and lived. Or perhaps, it was because he had proven the gingerbread people wrong. Clayton suddenly stopped laughing when he remembered what else the gingerbread people had said about the evil candy bears and their appetite.

Who are the candy bears? Clayton wondered.

Trying to shake the terrifying thought, Clayton got up and began walking yet again.

Clayton's stomach growled with hunger as he noticed a small blue pond at the side of the gingerbread path. When he approached the pond and leaned down, he realized that it wasn't filled with water.

"That shouldn't be a surprise," Clayton said out loud, referring to the not-so-normal pond. He felt a bit better when he heard the sound of his own voice.

Looking carefully into the dark blue pond, he saw chunks of floating ice. Confident that he knew what the pond contained, Clayton bent down and tasted the blueberry flavored slushy. Clayton felt overcome with joy as he stuck his face into the blue slushy pond and drank.

As he lifted his face out of the pond, he saw something in the distance that he hadn't noticed before. It looked like a frozen pond, only much larger than the one Clayton was kneeling over.

As Clayton advanced towards the pond, he realized it was indeed frozen. He also noticed how the pond was white with thin lines of red and green running throughout it.

"It looks like a gigantic candy cane ice rink!" Clayton exclaimed, while staring at the beauty and vastness of the rink.

Clayton saw the six stick figures first and then he heard the noise that they made as they glided towards him. Although he had seen strange things since arriving in the Kingdom of Sugar, these figures took the prize for the weirdest.

The candy cane people were about seven feet in height and were white with thin lines of red and green running through them. The figures had two arms that matched their body and large black eyes.

Clayton suddenly realized that he may be in danger. He turned around and prepared to run.

"Don't go," a voice that sounded as if he was talking through a pipe said.

Clayton turned around quickly to see that the candy cane people had a small slit for a mouth.

"Don't go," the candy cane person said again.

Clayton watched in amazement as the five other candy cane people nodded their heads in agreement.

"Are you guys good?" Clayton asked shakily. He watched in fear as two candy cane people hopped off the ice and went behind him. He panicked as they formed a circle around him. Clayton held his breath as one of the candy cane people drew his face close to his.

"Of course!" the candy cane person exclaimed, obviously pleased with himself for frightening Clayton.

Clayton let out a deep breath and then smiled. "So, you can tell me how to get home, right?"

One of the candy cane people looked Clayton up and down. "I knew you weren't from here!" he exclaimed. "We have a lot of different inhabitants in the Kingdom of Sugar, but no one who looks like you."

"Thanks...I think," Clayton said, not really sure if he should take that comment as a compliment or not. "Can you help me get home?" he asked, remembering why he was talking to the candy cane people in the first place.

"Do you want to play with us on our ice rink?" one of the candy cane people asked.

Why aren't they answering my question? Clayton wondered, his face flushing red with anger.

"Oh yes," another candy cane person replied enthusiastically. "Our new friend can be the goalie while the rest of us split up into teams of three."

All the other candy cane people nodded happily in agreement.

"But I want to go home," Clayton whined. He didn't care if he sounded like a baby; he really wanted to get away from all the weird creatures who resided in the Kingdom of Sugar.

"So you don't want to play with us?" one candy cane person asked sadly.

Not wanting to upset the candy cane people, Clayton put on, what he hoped was a pitiful face and sadly added, "I just want to go home."

"We'll help you if we can," a candy cane person said kindly. "Where is this place that you call home?"

"Earth," Clayton answered, wondering if he was still on Earth.

"Did you say Earth?" a candy cane person asked in shock.

"Yes," Clayton said, suddenly getting the dreadful feeling that he'd said the wrong thing.

"Are you a human?" one of the candy cane people whispered, as if not wanting anyone else to hear.

"Yes," Clayton repeated. As soon as the word had escaped his mouth, he regretted it.

The candy cane people licked their non-existent lips hungrily.

How could I forget that the inhabitants of the Kingdom of Sugar eat humans? Clayton scolded himself. "Well, thanks for inviting me to play with you, but I really should be going."

"Hold on a minute," a candy cane person said slyly.

"I really have to go," Clayton said, with rising panic.

"Just stay for one more minute," the sly candy cane person said again.

"No!" Clayton yelled, turning around and running as fast as he could towards the familiar gingerbread path.

As soon as he had returned to the gingerbread path, Clayton stopped for a quick breath and looked behind him. His whole body shook as he saw that the candy cane people were still running after him. Luckily, they couldn't move fast since they had no legs.

"So much for being good candy canes," Clayton said spitefully as he began to run again.

I've never had so much exercise in my life! Clayton thought as he looked behind once again. For some reason, the candy cane people looked a lot smaller. *I must be running a lot faster than them,* Clayton reasoned.

As he continued to run, Clayton kept looking behind. The candy cane people were close; however, they were also very small. Clayton's lungs ached and his legs began to develop cramps. He knew he was slowing down.

Soon, Clayton was too tired to run anymore. He slowed down to a jog and then finally to a slower pace.

I'll never make it, Clayton thought sadly as he looked behind one last time. What he saw made him laugh.

Running only a few feet behind Clayton were the seven foot candy cane people who had somehow shrunk to five inches tall.

"What happened to you guys?" Clayton asked in a baby voice.

The candy cane people jumped up and down in anger. They spoke, but since they were so small, Clayton couldn't hear what they were saying.

Clayton laughed loudly, hoping to annoy and deafen the candy cane people at the same time. He laughed again as he picked up one of the candy cane people and flung it off the gingerbread path. He did the same with the remaining five.

Clayton walked back down the path a little bit, trying to find what caused the candy cane people to shrink. He soon realized what had happened when he saw chips of candy cane scattered over the harsh gingerbread.

"They must have grated themselves on the gingerbread path," Clayton reasoned out loud. The smile, which had played upon his face for the last few minutes, disappeared as he thought about how the candy cane people had destroyed their lives by giving into temptation. "They just couldn't control their cravings for humans," he said sadly, while thinking of his own craving that had ruined his life.

Once Clayton had finished resting after the candy cane people incident, he began walking down the gingerbread path yet again. "I'm getting really sick of you," he foolishly told the path.

After half an hour of walking, Clayton came to the edge of a dark, dense forest. He gulped in fear at the scary scene. He was sure there would be equally scary creatures residing in there. However, since the gingerbread path went into the forest, Clayton was going there as well.

Clayton felt courage swell in his chest as he entered the forest. The thickness of the dark green cotton candy leaves easily blocked the brightness of the lollipop sun. Despite the fear of being in such a strange place, Clayton found himself in awe over the forest. The trunks of the gingerbread trees were massive. Even the silver balls that lined the gingerbread path were more abundant and shiny than the other ones Clayton had seen earlier.

As a soft breeze swept through the forest, Clayton blinked in surprise at what he saw. Every time a breeze blew, the cotton candy leaves would shake and then release green sparkly sugar everywhere. The scene was so beautiful that Clayton stopped walking and just stared at the glittering sugar as it fell to the ground.

A noise behind Clayton snapped him back to reality. He quickly glanced behind to see what was there. At first Clayton saw nothing, but when he looked down, he gasped in horror. There, only two feet away from him, was a black snake.

Clayton turned and ran in fear. He glanced back to see if the snake was following him. Upon realizing that the snake hadn't moved, Clayton stopped running and cautiously approached the snake. His heart raced; he had hated snakes for as long as he could remember. Clayton stood a few feet back from the snake as he eyed it suspiciously. Then suddenly, he burst out laughing.

Clayton relaxed as he realized that his "snake" was nothing more than a black string of licorice. *It must have fallen from a tree when the wind blew,* he thought, reaching for the licorice. *It's heavier than I thought it would be.*

Bringing the licorice closer to his face, Clayton saw no harm in taking a nibble. He could already taste the sugary goodness as he closed his eyes, parted his lips and prepared to take a bite.

Clayton's eyes flew open as he heard a hissing sound in front of his face. He screamed in horror when he saw two yellow eyes and a red tongue hissing violently.

Clayton dropped the licorice snake and then prepared to run. Unfortunately, he had dropped the snake too close to his feet. The snake had no problem wrapping himself tightly around Clayton's ankles. He tried to run, but instead fell to the ground in a heap. The hissing sound grew deafening as the licorice snake tightened his grip on Clayton.

Clayton felt his legs tingle as the snake continued to squeeze. *He's going to squeeze me to death then eat me,* Clayton realized in horror. As his legs went numb, Clayton knew he had to act now if he wanted to survive.

Struggling to get up, Clayton finally managed to sit upright by pulling on a nearby branch. With a cry that was full of pain and rage, he lunged forward and sank his teeth deep into the snake.

The licorice snake hissed angrily as he uncoiled himself from around Clayton's ankles. Finally, he slithered away into the darkness of the forest.

Clayton rubbed his throbbing ankles and waited for the blood to return to them. Slowly, feeling returned to his limbs.

Not knowing what else to do, Clayton shakily got on his feet and began walking deeper into the forest.

Clayton's feet ached and his stomach growled. He'd been walking for two hours since the snake attack. He had no idea where he was going or how to get out of the Kingdom of Sugar. The only thing he knew for sure was that he never wanted to see candy again.

"I wonder how long I'll survive out here," Clayton said, being only a little bit comforted by the sound of his voice.

Feeling completely exhausted and devoid of hope, Clayton stopped walking and sat on the hard gingerbread ground. Not really caring if anyone had ever walked on it before, he began chipping at the gingerbread ground and eating it. He had no desire for it but knew he must eat to sustain himself.

Clayton picked a few silver balls to eat and then leaned against a thick tree to rest. He felt his head nodding forward and his eyes getting heavier. Giving into temptation, he lay back on the ground.

Clayton had just gotten comfortable when he heard a weird noise. Exhausted, he ignored the noise until it grew louder and closer. It sounded like a child sloppily chewing on the stickiest candy ever created. Clayton opened his eyes and then let out a horrified scream.

In front of Clayton stood a large, yellow candy bear. The candy bear was a transparent yellow and only had indentations as features. Clayton gulped when he realized there were green, blue, purple and orange candy bears behind the yellow one. Although Clayton was terrified to see a group of candy bears, it was the one feature he hadn't seen until the candy bears opened their mouths that made him scream in terror. Every candy bear had two rows of razor sharp teeth.

"They always scream," the yellow candy bear remarked before leaping towards Clayton.

Clayton's cries for help were muffled as the candy bear opened his mouth and swallowed him whole. Clayton felt a coldness that chilled him to the bone as he traveled through the candy bear's body.

I've been eaten, Clayton realized in horror.

Clayton began kicking and thrashing in protest until he passed right through the candy bear.

Surprised, Clayton looked at his arms and legs to see them covered in sticky candy bear residue. He turned around to face the angry candy bears.

"Yuck!" the yellow candy bear cried, while holding his stomach as if he'd just eaten something bad.

Clayton tried to run away, but he was easily caught by a purple candy bear. The other bears surrounded him, all the while bearing their long, sharp teeth. Clayton stared in horror as they formed a tight circle around him and then attacked. All he could hear was a ringing in his ears.

The ringing grew louder until it became distinguishable as an alarm clock. Groaning, Clayton turned on his side to hit the sleep button. As soon as the ringing stopped, he sat straight up in bed. Fully awake, Clayton remembered his horrifying experience in the Kingdom of Sugar. He shivered with fear.

It was just a dream, Clayton told himself as he headed to the kitchen for breakfast. *But it seemed so real.*

"Clayton!" Mrs. Baxter shouted angrily when he entered the kitchen.

"What's wrong?"

"How could you?" Mrs. Baxter asked in disappointment. "After having that talk with you last night, I was certain you'd reduce your sugar intake."

Confused, Clayton looked into the small mirror that hung over the counter top. He gasped when he saw smears of gingerbread across his mouth. "The Kingdom of Sugar," he whispered in horror.

Mrs. Baxter sighed. "Clayton, you have to stop eating so many sugary treats. You've become obsessed! Promise me once and for all that you will never go to the Kingdom of Sugar again."

She thinks the Kingdom of Sugar is a candy store, Clayton realized. "I promise," he said solemnly. "Believe me, the Kingdom of Sugar is one place I never want to return to!"

As Clayton headed to the bathroom to wash his face, Mrs. Baxter smiled at him in relief. She was happy to see her son so determined to kick his bad habit.

Suddenly, Mrs. Baxter's eyebrows knitted in confusion as she spotted something on the floor. When she bent down and picked it up, she sighed in disappointment. She held a small yellow candy bear.

"I guess Clayton will need a lot of help," Mrs. Baxter muttered.

"I'll take care of him," a small, sinister voice said.

Mrs. Baxter looked at the candy bear in her hand and screamed.

* * *

125

About the Author

Heather Beck is a Canadian author and screen-writer who began writing professionally at the age of sixteen. Her first book was published when she was only nineteen years old. Since then she has written several well-reviewed books.

Heather recently received an Honors Bachelor of Arts from university where she specialized in English and studied an array of disciplines. Currently, she is working on two young adult novels and has six anthologies slated for publication. As a screenwriter, Heather has multiple television shows and movies in development. Her short films include *Young Eyes* and *The Rarity*.

Besides writing, Heather's greatest passion is the outdoors. She is an award-winning fisher-woman and a regular hiker. Her hobbies include swimming, playing badminton and volunteering with non-profit organizations.